I0721553

HONEY BEAR COSY MYSTERIES

HONEY MOON MURDER

DAHLIA DONOVAN

HOT TREE PUBLISHING

ALSO BY DAHLIA DONOVAN

THE GRASMERE COTTAGE MYSTERY TRILOGY

DEAD IN THE GARDEN | DEAD IN THE POND | DEAD IN THE SHOP

MOTTS COLD CASE MYSTERY SERIES

POISONED PRIMROSE | PIERCED PEONY | PICKLED PETUNIA | PURLOINED POINSETTIA

LONDON PODCAST MYSTERY SERIES

COSPLAY KILLER | GHOST LIGHT KILLER | CROWN COURT KILLER

HONEY BEAR COSY MYSTERIES

HONEY MEAD MURDER | HONEY BEE MURDER | HONEY MOON MURDER

STAND-ALONE ROMANCES

AFTER THE SCRUM | AT WAR WITH A BROKEN HEART | FORGED IN FLOOD | FOUND YOU | ONE LAST HEIST | PURE DUMB LUCK | HERE COMES THE SON | ALL LATHERED UP | NOT EVEN A MOUSE | FARM TO FABRE | THE MISGUIDED CONFESSION | STUBBED TOES & DATING WOES

THE SIN BIN (COMPLETE SERIES)

The Wanderer | The Caretaker | The Royal Marine | The Botanist | The Unexpected Santa | The Lion Tamer | Haka Ever After

HONEY MOON MURDER

HONEY BEAR COSY MYSTERIES
BOOK 3

DAHLIA DONOVAN

TANGLED TREE PUBLISHING

Honey Moon Murder © 2024 by Dahlia Donovan

All rights reserved. No part of this book may be used or reproduced in any written, electronic, recorded, or photocopied format without the express permission from the author or publisher as allowed under the terms and conditions with which it was purchased or as strictly permitted by applicable copyright law. Any unauthorized distribution, circulation or use of this text may be a direct infringement of the author's rights, and those responsible may be liable in law accordingly. Thank you for respecting the work of this author.

Honey Moon Murder is a work of fiction. All names, characters, events and places found therein are either from the author's imagination or used fictitiously. Any similarity to persons alive or dead, actual events, locations, or organizations is entirely coincidental and not intended by the author.

For information, contact the publisher, Tangled Tree Publishing.

www.Tangledtreepublishing.com

Editing: Hot Tree Editing

Cover Designer: BooksSmith Design

E-book ISBN: 978-1-922679-78-9

Paperback ISBN: 978-1-922679-79-6

For Bacon, who I miss every day.

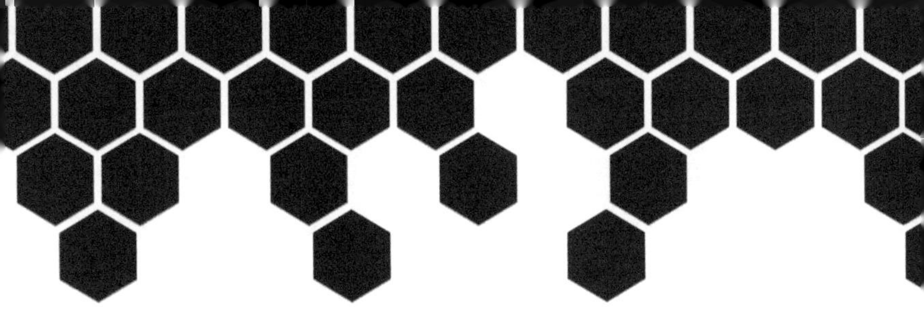

ONE
GEORGE

"Moon's out." Margo lazily raised her arm to point up into the midnight sky. "Days are finally starting to get shorter again. We're ready for the steep descent into autumn."

"Yes, that's what happens in August." George smothered a yawn into his shoulder, unable to move his hands since his elderly pug, Bumble, and Margo's Chihuahua, Treacle, had taken up possession of them and his lap in general. The two pups were the best of friends. "I'm glad. It's been a bizarre summer. Dead bodies practically falling out of the sky."

"There were two murders. A month apart. And neither body fell out of the sky." Margo poked a hole in his dramatic retelling. "It hasn't been all bad. You've finally admitted to being in love with Murphy

Baird. You're moving in together. I've started dating Teagan. We've had good things this summer. Don't let your mind trick you into focusing on the bad."

"My mind is not always my best friend." George accepted and appreciated all the quirks that made up who he was. But there were times when being autistic added additional hurdles to his life. "It does make things interesting, though."

It had been a busy summer for George Bernard Sheth. Maybe the most active since he'd moved from Edinburgh to a little cottage in Dufftown, where he'd created his perfect wild garden, complete with multiple beehives. They were his greatest passion.

The swarming had died down at the end of July. He'd spend August harvesting honey and preparing his colonies for the onset of the cooler months. It was a routine he knew well after several years of tending to his bees.

Closing his eyes momentarily, George allowed himself to enjoy the calm of Margo's garden. His cousin didn't go beyond their cosy little corner of the village often and rarely got into a car, still struggling with post-traumatic stress brought on by an accident during her time as a paramedic. They visited each other daily since he lived just down the lane.

They shared their love of gardens and calm,

along with the thick black hair and deep brown eyes inherited from their fathers. The Sheth brothers had moved from Udaipur to Edinburgh with their parents years ago, but his uncle had been the one to move to Dufftown. His mum and dad had remained in the larger city, preferring it to quiet village life.

"You're due a cut." Margo interrupted his thoughts.

George reached up to clasp the end of his ponytail. "Back, demon."

"I'm serious. It's longer than you usually let it get." Margo laughed when he tried to fend her off with a made-up prayer. "George."

"Margo." He hated having his hair trimmed, often going years between cuts to avoid the experience. He occasionally tried to do it himself. "My heart weeps for your lack of empathy."

"Weep all you want, you know I'm right. Isn't your dad coming for a visit again soon? Why don't you see if Teagan's auntie will trim it for you? I bet they'd get her to open early so you didn't have to deal with masses of people."

George shrugged. He ran his fingers across Bumble's head. "I'll give them a call later. Or... maybe you could ask?"

"Buzz."

George couldn't help teasing his cousin, who'd started dating Teagan around the same time he'd finally dared to do more than crush on Murphy from afar. They worked at the brewery and had moved to Dufftown to be closer to their aunt. "You see them more than I do or even Murphy, and he's their employer."

"I'm ignoring you now," Margo huffed. She made sure to chuckle so he knew she wasn't really upset.

"I should head home. It's getting late. I want to get up early to put the blocks into the hives and help deter wasps. And I've got to finally take care of the empty patch in my garden." George had been putting it off for weeks. He'd ruined his lavender patch when a killer had been chasing after him. "I need to get my plans together for autumn and winter."

"How are you doing? Still having nightmares?"

"No. Maybe." George had initially had them every night after his close brush with death. They'd finally begun to trail off, though. "Murphy helps."

"Yes, a big strong bear of a man in bed would do wonders." Margo winked. She laughed when he threw a handful of grass in her direction. "Did you talk to the therapist I recommended?"

"I did."

"Good." Margo had gently nudged him towards speaking to someone about what had happened. She'd even managed to find one who had experience with neurodivergent clients. It made his visits much simpler. "Want to take some of the muffins I baked home?"

"Hmm?" George needed a second to process the question. He nodded before she could repeat herself. "Just a couple. Murphy said he'd bring breakfast. He's staying at his flat over the brewery tonight."

"One last night?"

"He's got some special mead that he's working on. It's delicate." George gently shifted the two pups in his lap. He set them both down on the grass and got to his feet. "We're taking the moving in slowly. My cottage is bigger than his tiny flat above the brewery, but combining two sets of things takes some finagling."

"Cold feet?"

George glanced down at his favourite socks poking out from the top of his trainers. "No, fairly warm."

"Not... never mind, not important. Let me put some of these muffins in a bag for you." Margo followed him into her cottage. She found a paper bag from one of the local bakeries and began filling it.

She channelled a lot of her bad days into baking. "Here. They'll be delicious in the morning for breakfast."

"You're my favourite cousin." George clutched the bag to his chest. He ignored her complaints about being his only cousin and went outside with Bumble trundling after him. "Ready to go home?"

His little pug peered up at him, wiggling a little in excitement. They headed down the path until they reached the lane. George glanced up at the full moon overhead; it was a clear and beautiful late-summer night.

Before George could head to the right, Bumble veered off to the left. He whistled for him, but there was no reaction. His pup kept plodding along without a response.

"Come on, Bumble Bee," George encouraged. He frowned when his dog continued in the opposite direction of his cottage. "Oi. Where are you going?"

For an elderly and partially blind pug, Bumble made swift progress moving away from him. George jogged to catch up. He stumbled to a halt when he found his dog sniffing at a lump in the middle of the lane.

Even with the bright moonlight, George needed a second to understand what he was seeing. A body.

Not a lump. Bumble had found what appeared to be a dead woman in the middle of a lane.

Oh, for… no one's ever going to believe this.

How?

How does this keep happening?

Rushing forward, George lifted Bumble into his arms and staggered back from the dead body in the lane. He scrambled into his pocket for his phone. His mind went blank while he stared at the list of favourite contacts on the screen.

Calm down.

Calm down.

They don't arrest dogs for murder.

It seemed a ridiculous thing to worry about. Still, George had just weeks earlier had his own brush with being considered a murder suspect. He wasn't taking any chances. His first call was to the police, the second to his solicitor, Evan Chan, and the third to his boyfriend, Murphy, who promised to be there in minutes.

The local constables arrived fairly quickly. They moved him further back from the body. Murphy came next. Detective Elwin Smith showed up at the exact same time as Evan.

It would've been amusing if George hadn't been terrified of being accused of murder. Elwin spoke briefly to Constable Sean Davie and his partner, Natalie Bettley. He could only clutch Bumble in his arms and wait.

"George." Elwin finally approached him after several minutes of conversation. "What happened?"

"I swear Bumble didn't kill anybody."

Elwin covered his face with his hand. He turned his head away and coughed a few times. George thought it was odd how often he had to clear his throat. "Can you tell me what happened?"

"Are you sick? I've got a throat lozenge in my pocket." George paused when Elwin shook his head. "Right. I was at Margo's all evening. I left maybe ten or twenty minutes ago. Not so great with estimating time. But Bumble took off in the wrong direction. I followed him and found him standing beside the body. He didn't kill anyone. And I didn't touch the person. At all. Not a finger went near them."

"Okay. Okay. I'm not accusing you or Bumble of anything." Elwin held his hands up, trying to calm him down a little. He peered over his shoulder, then back at George. "You called your solicitor first?"

"Technically, second. I called the police first. And in my defence, twice now, I've seen false accusations of murder. Murphy and then myself. I'm not jumping up and down to find myself in the middle of a third." George once again gestured to the dog in his arms. "Bumble didn't murder anyone."

"Of course he didn't." Detective Inspector Elwin Smith rubbed his forehead and sighed exhaustedly. "If I'd moved to Keith, I wouldn't be the first person on the scene, and you'd be someone else's problem. You'd be Sarah's issue for the night. Do you happen to recognise the victim?"

George shook his head so quickly that his hair smacked his cheeks. "Never seen them before that I can tell. I didn't exactly do a study on their face."

"Right." Elwin heaved yet another deep sigh. "All right. Just... go home and try to avoid any other dead bodies."

"I wasn't trying to find this one." George shoved his hair out of his face. He couldn't wait to be safely home with a warm cup of tea. Murphy could help him make sense of everything.

TWO

MURPHY

WHAT IN THE DEVIL IS HAPPENING IN DUFFTOWN?

It was the first thought to pop into his mind when George called about finding a body. Again. How had it happened three months in a row? It was definitely the most murder-filled summer Murphy could ever recall happening in their little Scottish village.

Ever.

Before the bizarre death by dry ice that happened in June in his brewery, Murphy genuinely couldn't remember the last time a murder had occurred in Dufftown. And then July had brought an allergy-induced murder. So he'd hoped August wouldn't bring more of the same.

Three times was apparently not the charm.

Murphy arrived to find the lane already blocked off by a police vehicle. He nodded to one of the constables, who asked him to stay where he was. George was further down the lane, holding Bumble tightly in his arms. *Bugger.*

It was several minutes before one of the local detective inspectors arrived. Thankfully for all of them, it was Elwin, not Murphy's cousin Sarah. She'd threatened to lock him up on principle if he got involved in another murder inquiry.

She was mostly joking.

He hoped.

For over an hour, Murphy had to stay by his vehicle and wait. It was painful to be unable to stand beside George and offer comfort. Finally, though, Elwin stepped over to speak with him.

"Paddy." Elwin acknowledged him with a nod.

Paddington had been his nickname since his very brief stint in the military. A moniker that was bestowed on him because of his Baird surname and overall tall, stocky build. The dark brown hair and scruffy beard didn't help matters much. It was a name that had stuck with him over the years.

"Everything all right?" Murphy glanced between the detective inspector and George. "You can't possibly think...."

"I don't believe George or his ancient pug was involved in this murder. We're fairly confident the murder happened several hours ago. Margo has one of those fancy doorbells with a camera. It shows when he left the cottage." Elwin held a hand up when Murphy when to interrupt him. "Give me some credit. I never believed he was involved in the last one either. We still have to do our job as investigators. So do me a favour, and don't poke around in the inquiry. I'm begging you to stay out of this one."

"I didn't intend to be in the other ones." Murphy held his hands up in surrender when Elwin glowered at him. "I'll do my best."

"You didn't intend...." Elwin muttered a few impressive curses under his breath, along with a prayer to any divine being listening. "Three times is not the charm. So let us handle this murder inquiry."

"To be fair, the last one literally fell into our laps. And we didn't investigate." Murphy grinned when his old schoolmate glowered at him even more deeply. "We didn't investigate much."

"Well, how about you go from not investigating much to not doing it at all? Now go take care of your boyfriend." Elwin carefully ushered Murphy around the victim, who was being placed into a body bag by the coroner. He narrowed his eyes at the two of them. "Behave yourselves."

Murphy waved off Elwin. It was sometimes hard to take him seriously when he'd known the man so long. He focused on an exhausted George, who still clutched a squirming Bumble in his arms. "Here. Why don't I walk you home? I'm sure you could use a break from the flashing lights and noise."

With a nod of acceptance, George wordlessly allowed Murphy to take Bumble. They walked away from the scene. He'd parked his vehicle off the side and out of the way; it would be fine until the police wrapped up their investigation.

A sharp whistle drew his attention to Evan, who stood by his vehicle. He promised to swing by George's cottage midmorning. They were definitely going to need to have a chat about anything their solicitor friend uncovered.

They weren't investigating.

They weren't.

It was just a few questions to a solicitor friend to see where the police inquiry might go. A protective measure, nothing more. He wasn't sure his argument would stand up in court or to the detectives.

Halfway to the cottage, Murphy set Bumble down to let him trundle along beside them. He'd been clutched in George's arms for quite a while. With the pug leading the way, they slowly walked towards the cottage at the end of the lane.

"I genuinely thought we were finished with dead bodies." George stopped in front of his cottage and spoke for the first time. He tilted his head to peer up at the sky. "Beautiful night. Moon's bright. A cool breeze. Everything's perfect—aside from the dead body."

"Pesky thing, those dead bodies." Murphy slipped his hand into George's, trying to offer him a measure of support. "At least they can't pin this one on you or me."

"What about Bumble?"

"Well, unless the person was snored or licked to death, I think he's in the clear." Murphy tried to inject a little humour into the situation to ease George's anxiety. "Why don't I fix us some of the calming tea your ma sent you?"

It was a delicious blend, particularly when paired with one of George's honey syrup experiments. His latest was a mixture containing blackberries and spices. It went surprisingly well in tea.

"Not sure tea's up to the task of calming me after Bumble found a body in the lane."

"Okay, first, sacrilege. They might chase you out

of the village if anyone hears you. Second, it could always be worse." Murphy took him by the shoulders and guided him up the path to the cottage. "He might've found two bodies."

"Ah, yes. Of course, the silver lining is that my elderly, half-blind pug found one murdered person and not two." George's smile was slightly tremulous, but it was there. "I'm exhausted, but I don't think I could sleep if I tried."

"Let's start with something manageable. Tea. You never know how you'll feel after you've had a cup." Murphy continued to guide George into the cottage and finally to one of the chairs at the kitchen table. "Are you hungry?"

George shook his head. He stared blankly at the top of the table, not even noticing Bumble, who flopped across his feet. "Not hungry."

After filling the kettle and turning it on, Murphy gathered two mugs, the box of tea, and the bottle of syrup. He left George to sift through his thoughts in silence. It was always best not to force him to speak when he was lost in thought.

Murphy grabbed the Loch Ness monster-shaped metal strainers and filled them with tea. He set them into the mugs, poured the hot water in, and chuckled at the little head bobbing at the top. The two were a set he'd gotten George as a gift.

After allowing the tea to brew for several minutes, Murphy took the strainers out and placed them in the sink. He added a little of the honey syrup and stirred it in. George nodded his thanks when Murphy set the tea in front of him.

George swirled the spoon around in the mug absently. "I wonder who the person was. I didn't recognise her. Not someone from around the village."

"Maybe a tourist? There was that wedding earlier. Teagan mentioned their auntie had the bridal party at the hair salon a few days earlier." Murphy sat down across from him. He cupped his hands around the mug, enjoying the warmth from it. "She could've been one of the guests who decided to stay past the ceremony and reception. Or someone just passing by? Maybe a hiker?"

"In the middle of the night?"

"It's still summer. It wouldn't be a complete stretch to have someone hiking through the highlands, maybe lost track of time." Murphy thought it unlikely, but it was possible. He noticed a jar with bright yellowish-orange contents on the counter. "Ah. Your new experiment? How'd it go?"

"Too soon to tell. I added a few spices to the honey and ginger. I went with cardamom, cinnamon, and nutmeg. I think it'll be quite lovely in the autumn. Something different to the fruity flavours I've played with this summer." George finally stopped stirring his tea and took a sip. He seemed happy enough with how Murphy had made it. "Are you hungry?"

"I could eat."

"I'm craving french toast." George continued drinking his tea before setting the mug down. "Craving Abba's french toast, to be specific."

"Not his pancakes?" Murphy had tried quite a few of the Sheth patriarch's creations. He was an amazing cook who blended Indian flavours into almost every dish. "What goes into the french toast, then?"

"A lot of spices and chilli." George closed his eyes for a moment. "In the morning. I'll make it in the morning before I head into the garden. I'm so tired all of a sudden."

"Come on. Let's finish up the tea and head for bed." Murphy found a container of cardamom-spiced shortbread and slid it across the table to George. "A little something to soothe the stomach beast."

"You'll stay?"

"Where else would I go?"

They finished up their tea in a silence punctuated by pug snores. Murphy could see the exhaustion slowly descending on George. He was practically asleep at the table by the time Murphy had washed up the mugs and teapot, setting them aside to dry overnight.

"Up you get. Your back won't thank you for falling asleep in your kitchen chair." Murphy went over to lift George up, who batted his hands away with a strained laugh. "Let's at least try to get some sleep, yeah?"

"Yeah." George's agreement was half-hearted at best.

Part of him wanted to carry George upstairs. But Murphy knew his boyfriend, no matter how tired, wouldn't appreciate that level of help. He followed closely to make sure George didn't stumble on the stairs.

He wasn't only tired but distracted. Who could blame him? For the third time in three months, they'd found themselves somehow connected or adjacent to a murder.

With stilted movements, George changed into a pair of shorts and collapsed on the bed with a tired sigh. He didn't even bother to get under the covers. His head missed the pillow entirely, but he didn't move.

Murphy undressed and pulled on a pair of pyjama bottoms. He gently shifted George until his head rested on the pillow and got him under the covers. Bumble huffed at him, wanting up on the bed, so he lifted the pug as well. "We'll take good care of him, right?"

Bumble immediately scrambled up to curl up on the pillow beside George's head. He seemed to agree wholeheartedly with the idea. Murphy watched for a moment before climbing into bed as well.

The quiet usually was peaceful in the cottage. However, Murphy could see the tension in George's body even in the dimly lit room. He definitely hadn't slipped off to sleep as quickly as the now-snoring Bumble.

George finally twisted around to face him. He shuffled forward a little until they could wrap their arms around each other. It took a moment to find a comfortable position. "Why would someone do that? Kill somebody and leave them in the lane like a bit of rubbish? It's so cold and callous. They just abandoned her in the street. How long was she there?"

"I don't know, Buzz." Murphy brought a hand up

to play with George's hair briefly. He didn't do it for long, knowing it could go from relaxing to annoying quickly. "I'll never understand how someone can take a life."

George mumbled something under his breath that Murphy couldn't quite hear. He shifted against him. "Never."

Murphy lowered his hand, adjusting his hold as George drifted off beside him. "Goodnight, Buzz."

THREE

GEORGE

Sunlight streamed into the bedroom at five in the morning. George whined in annoyance at himself for forgetting to close the curtains. Finally, he forced his eyes open.

Why am I so tired?

It hit him all of a sudden when Bumble snuffled in his ear. Their late-night walk had turned into yet another misadventure. He rubbed his eyes tiredly and tried to shake off the remnants of a dream.

Bumble slid further down the pillow until his little face smashed against George's cheek. He wriggled around until his paw could reach him—a definite sign that the pug wanted outside.

"Is it garden time?" George chuckled when Bumble wiggled excitedly. "All right. Up we go."

Carefully plucking Bumble off his shoulder, George slipped from under Murphy's arm. He held his breath, hoping they hadn't woken the man. However, the continued snoring told him it was safe to escape.

Setting Bumble on the floor, George grabbed a T-shirt and pulled it on. He headed out of the bedroom, downstairs, and into the garden with Bumble at his heels. The cool breeze hit him immediately and sent a shiver up his spine.

The summer had been mostly mild, with the occasional exceptionally boiling days. But a few days into August, it had gone from warmer than usual to a cold snap. He regretted not grabbing his dressing gown or a cardigan, something more than shorts and a T-shirt.

Bumble appeared to agree with his assessment. He quickly retraced his steps, wanting back into the cottage. George picked up the black-and-yellow-striped cardigan his aunt had knitted for him a while ago and the little pack of grooming wipes.

"Now, now, don't grumble at me. We have to keep all your wrinkles clean." George snatched a soft cloth off a nearby shelf and gently wiped Bumble's eyes as well. He slipped the cardigan on the pug once he'd finished. "There. How about we find breakfast?"

The urge to make french toast had died with his early wake-up. George got the water boiling for coffee and fixed breakfast for Bumble first. The basket of muffins caught his attention on the counter.

In all of the chaos, George was honestly surprised they made it home safely. He'd forgotten he even had them. They'd be an excellent start to breakfast, if nothing else.

Two muffins and a mug of coffee later, George was at least somewhat more awake. Bumble had finished his meal and collapsed on the nearest blanket for his early-morning nap. It gave George time to think through what he needed to accomplish.

His camera sat charging on the kitchen counter. He needed to film a video for his YouTube channel. It had started picking up traction in the past couple of weeks.

Several of his friends within the beekeeping community online had asked him to make a video about his end-of-summer tasks. He'd done a part one at the beginning of August. Being on camera still made him uncomfortable, but he enjoyed sharing what he'd learnt over the years.

There was also the empty patch where his

lavender had once been. He kept going back and forth on what he wanted to do. His initial thoughts had been to simply replace the ruined plants.

But there were other lavender patches, so it wouldn't be completely absent. He'd made a list of pollinating plants, trying to decide which to choose. It had to complement the wild, chaotic approach to his garden.

Grabbing his gardening and bee journal, George flipped to the current month. He eyed the sketches he'd made for the patch. There was enough space that he considered planting a winter honeysuckle shrub or a patch of Michaelmas daisies, both plants he hadn't dabbled with previously.

He was leaning towards the latter. Michaelmas daisies had such beautiful colours. He'd likely go with one of the blue or purple varieties.

Taking his pen, George jotted down Professor Kippenburg. It was one of the taller daisy varieties in a stunning purple and yellow. They'd make the perfect addition to his wild secret garden.

George flipped back a few pages to where he kept his long-term plans. He scribbled in a note to explore a full daisy section the year after next. Of course, there were other things he wanted to do first, but he tended to forget if he didn't write ideas down.

Once finished, George put his journal aside. He enjoyed his quiet mornings. One of his fears around Murphy moving in had been that his routine might be completely disrupted.

His greatest tool for managing some of his stress as an autistic was keeping to a schedule. It helped him stay on track and not get overwhelmed. Introducing Murphy into the mix would obviously change things.

It had to, no matter how much Murphy promised to adapt. That hadn't seemed fair for his boyfriend to do more of the compromising. George had been reassured by his dad that making adjustments was a normal part of a relationship.

He hadn't always had the best of luck when it came to relationships until Murphy. It had been part of the reason he'd been content to crush from afar. But waking up next to the man he loved had thus far been worth the upheaval.

"What do you think, Bumble? Should we keep him around?" George chuckled when his pug barely acknowledged his words. "If you think we should, snore loudly. Excellent, you agree."

"Our Bumble Bee is quite the conversationalist early in the morning." Murphy came down the stairs. He had George's plush dressing gown in hand.

"Thought you might want this. We've had a bit of chill descend on us."

"Figuratively and literally." George slipped on the dressing gown and enjoyed the warmth of it. "There's muffins in the basket and coffee, though it's *not* in the basket."

"Good to know." Murphy caught the sleeve of the robe and drew George into a hug. "You all right?"

"Mostly. A wee cottony in my head." George usually described the odd spacy feeling after a particularly overwhelming day as having cotton shoved into his ears. "I can't help wondering if the police are going to be banging down the door to arrest me."

"Or Bumble." Murphy always seemed to know when to interject a dose of humour to derail his panicked spiral. "I believe we're safe. The only invasion we're going to have is Teagan and Evan, who will undoubtedly want to rehash every single moment from last night."

"And probably Margo."

"And probably Margo, but your cousin will likely bring food." Murphy made an excellent point.

To both of their surprise, it was Detective Inspector Sarah Baird who showed up at the cottage first. She'd come in her personal vehicle without her partner. George chose to take those things as an encouraging sign.

"Morning, cousin." Murphy dragged Sarah into a backbreaking hug, letting her go when she punched him in the chest. "What brings you out here so early?"

"I brought brekkie. Ma made these last night." Sarah offered up the container of what appeared to be breakfast pies. "Can we have a natter?"

"Isn't bribery illegal?" Murphy grabbed the container from her. "But I won't say no to food."

Dodging by the two cousins, George let them talk. He returned to the kitchen for a second mug of coffee. The day was clearly going to require more caffeine.

All of the caffeine.

Slumping into one of the chairs at the kitchen table, George sipped his fresh cup of coffee. He barely acknowledged the cousins when they joined him. Murphy rested a hand on his shoulder, then took a seat beside him.

"I'm not here in an official capacity. Well, not entirely," Sarah reassured them both. She gratefully accepted a mug of coffee for herself. "Elwin filled me in on what happened overnight. You'll be pleased to know neither you nor Bumble are suspects. Margo's

Ring camera shows when you arrived and left her cottage. We have a time of death that puts you firmly at her place, plus we believe the victim died elsewhere."

"So someone dumped her on the lane?" Murphy opened the lid of the container, took one of the pies, and slid it over to George. "Any idea who she was?"

"Valerie Collins. Newly married to her wife, Cara Larkin. They had their wedding here two days ago and stayed for their honeymoon. Several of the guests also remained in the village." Sarah held up her hand when George went to ask a question. "I can't tell you anything more than I've already said."

"Valerie Collins. The name doesn't sound familiar to me." George decided not to say much else. Sarah didn't need to know they'd planned to ask Teagan's auntie if she remembered anything about the bridal party. He slid the basket on the table. "Muffin?"

"No, I've got to get going." Sarah drained the last of her coffee. "I wanted to relieve any anxiety you might have over the investigation."

George wasn't entirely certain she'd relieved his anxiety, but he nodded anyway. "Thank you."

FOUR

MURPHY

Murphy followed his cousin to the front door. He had a feeling she'd kept something back. "Sarah? Something you want to share with your favourite relative?"

"Sure. Where are they?"

"You're not even half as funny as you think you are." Murphy rolled his eyes when she practically cackled at him. "What's going on? You've gone all twitchy like when you stole Granny Baird's purse."

"I borrowed it."

Murphy shook his head at her. "Terrible behaviour for a detective inspector."

"I was four."

"Sad to see a life of crime started so young."

Murphy grunted when she elbowed him in the stom-ach. "Oi."

Sarah's laughter faded away after a moment. "Listen, Paddy, I want you to keep an eye on George."

"Okay." He was immediately suspicious. "Why?"

"We live in a small village."

"And the sky is blue. What's your point?" Murphy stepped out of the cottage with her, following her down the path to where her vehicle was parked. "Sarah? Either tell me or don't. You can't give me half the story."

"The widow is a little emotionally distraught."

"Understandable given the circumstances." Murphy could only imagine how losing a spouse days or hours after marrying them might overwhelm someone. "What does it have to do with George?"

"Distraught and under the impression George might've done more than stumble upon a body." Sarah immediately held a hand up to stop Murphy from defending his boyfriend. "Not a rumour I've shared or Elwin. We haven't released any informa-tion. We've barely begun our investigation. Someone mentioned he found the victims, and I'd wager the widow became fixated."

"Distraught and fixated? Has she threatened him?"

"Not to my knowledge. I only wanted you to be aware. And I plan on speaking with her this morning to correct any misunderstanding. You know how gossip goes in our wee little village." Sarah did have a point. He'd seen how things spread from one person to the next. "Stay out of trouble."

There was no doubt in his mind that "stay out of trouble" actually meant "keep away from my investigation." Murphy nodded his agreement. He had no intentions of bungling through yet another police inquiry.

After Sarah had driven off, Murphy heard the door open. Bumble trundled down the path to plop down at his feet. George joined them a second after.

"Evan texted me to see if we were awake. He's coming over to chat. I mentioned Sarah's visit." George had changed into jeans and a long-sleeved T-shirt. He still had a mug of coffee in one hand. "You'd think a solicitor wouldn't be quite so excitable at seven in the morning."

"Probably dealing with uncooperative clients." Murphy had no doubts Evan would be annoyed at their willingly speaking with Sarah, despite her promises of George not being a suspect. "He'll be fine."

"I'm going to garden. Alone."

Without another word, George disappeared back into the cottage. Bumble remained at Murphy's feet. He glanced between the pug and the house, shaking his head and laughing.

There were times when George managed to blend perfectly into the neurotypical world. But other times, he didn't appear aware of social niceties. He was never rude on purpose, just oblivious to the necessity of certain parts of conversation.

Things Murphy knew instinctually never even occurred to George. It was refreshing. And on occasion, it could be amusing.

Murphy never took it personally. Because it wasn't. "Well, Bumble? Why don't we whip up something more substantial for breakfast than a muffin? Fancy a wee sausage?"

Taking the enthusiastic wiggling as a yes, Murphy strode back into the cottage with Bumble at his heels. He spied George through the window, checking on a section of his garden. It would likely be hours before he came up for air.

There was a knock on the door before Murphy could grab anything from the fridge. A frantic series of them. He opened it to find a tall brunette with windswept hair and red-rimmed eyes on the other side.

"Yes?" Murphy had never seen the woman before. She reared back with her arm in the air as if she'd been about to knock again. "Did you want something?"

"Where is he? Where's the bastard who killed my wife?" She launched herself forward, but Murphy caught her by the wrists and held her away from him. "Where is he?"

"Calm yourself down. No one in this cottage harmed your wife. He found her. She was already dead—had been for several hours." Murphy sighed when she shook her head violently, disagreeing with him. "You can argue all you like. There's CCTV footage proving I'm right. Where's your family?"

"He...."

Murphy kept a tight grip on her arms, holding her away from his body. He regretted answering the door. "Where's your family? Are you here by yourself?"

To his immense relief, another vehicle came down the lane while he continued trying to calm the woman down. He recognised Elwin's car. It didn't matter why the detective inspector was there; he only cared about handing off the obviously grieving widow to someone else.

Anyone else.

"Paddy?" Elwin had leapt out of his vehicle and rushed up the path, obviously noticing him restraining the woman. "Need a hand?"

"Maybe two." Murphy didn't want to hurt the bereaved woman, but he wasn't going to let her anywhere near George. "She appears to be distraught and confused."

"Ms Larkin?" Elwin gently extracted her from Murphy. He guided her down the path away from the cottage. "We spoke earlier. The murder inquiry has only started, but I can say with absolute certainty that neither Murphy nor George had anything to do with it."

"But...."

"Without George, we might not have found your wife before morning." Elwin managed to get her into his vehicle. He sent Murphy an apologetic grimace. "I'll give you a call."

"Fair enough." Murphy sighed. He stood, watching them drive up the lane and out of sight. *Why do I get the feeling this is going to get far more complicated?*

The door behind him opened. He heard the

scrambling of Bumble, who plopped down next to him. George followed a moment after, halfway dressed in his beekeeping gear.

"Everything all right? I heard knocking."

Murphy didn't want to make George even more anxious, but he also knew it was better to be honest. "The widow decided to track us down. Elwin happened to show up with impeccable timing for once. He'll set her straight."

"She thought I killed her wife?"

"We corrected her." Murphy wasn't entirely certain Ms or Mrs or whatever Larkin had believed him and Elwin. Time would tell. "I'd like to know how she knew about you."

"Maybe she killed her wife?"

"What?" Murphy glanced over to where George had gone to inspect the mixture of verbena and thyme in front of the cottage. "You think the wife did it?"

"Maybe. I agree it's odd she knew to come here. How? I doubt the police would've mentioned it. Village gossip is fast, but... it's still strange. Could she have seen me find the body?" George had clearly been thinking about it. "Don't killers return to the scene?"

"I imagine it's something the police will ask her."

Murphy could see the wheels turning in George's mind. He had no doubts about what his boyfriend was thinking. "We promised not to get involved."

"Think they might involve us whether we want to be or not." George did have an excellent point. "We'll play it by ear."

"So, I shouldn't have Teagan and Margo swing by so we can ask them about the bridal party who stopped by their auntie's hair salon?" Murphy laughed when George whipped around to glare in his direction. "They're already on their way. Evan's texted me. He'll be late. "

"Evan's going to be annoyed we spoke with Sarah."

"Evan's annoyed when we breathe in the direction of the police." Murphy couldn't necessarily blame their solicitor friend, who'd already had to represent them when they'd been accused of murder. "Not sure why he grumbles. We're keeping him in business all on our own."

They were still joking about Evan when Margo and Teagan strolled up with an excited Treacle at their feet. The Chihuahua raced forward to join Bumble in a chaotic dance around the garden. The two flopped down together once their best friend greeting had finished.

"You'd think they hadn't seen each other in years." Margo had a tight hold of Teagan's hand.

It was good to see their relationship deepen. Murphy thought Teagan might be good for Margo, who'd hidden away from the world after the incident that ended her career as a paramedic. Maybe it would give her back some confidence.

"Auntie Irie sends her love. She's off to Edinburgh for some shopping, but she gave me all the details about the bridal party." Teagan lifted up the container in their hand. "She also made those banana fritters you love."

Murphy restrained himself from snatching it from them. "Did she?"

Teagan smirked before handing the container over. "Enjoy. I've had breakfast. And I know your lust for the little fritters is legendary."

The banana fritters were a family recipe that went back to Jamaica. The sweet ripe bananas mixed with brown sugar, spices, and flour and then deep-fried. They were delicious, and Murphy could eat a thousand of them.

"So, what bits of gossip has Auntie Irie gathered up for us?" Murphy pried the lid off the container. He tossed it to Teagan, who snickered at him before he grabbed one of the fritters and shoved it whole into his mouth. "We had a visit from a Ms or Mrs Larkin—the grieving widow."

"Did you? I thought I spied someone storming down the lane earlier." Teagan tried to swipe one of the fritters, but he held the container over their head. "Don't be a greedy prick. And it's Cara Larkin. Her wife was Valerie Collins. They were all staying at the SB Bed and Breakfast."

"I'm telling Sky and Brannon that you've bastardised their name again." Murphy had finally lowered the container so they could have a fritter of their own. "Cara and Valerie."

"Apparently, a cousin, brother, and a few friends are still in the village. Most are staying at the bed and breakfast. A few rented an Airbnb together." Teagan handed the container over when he held his hand out. They stood outside the cottage, snacking on the fritters and chatting. "If we finish these before Margo and George get one, I'm blaming you."

"Fair enough. What about Cara Larkin?"

"Auntie Irie says the brides seemed very in love. There was a little mouse of a cousin who stayed off to one side through the entire visit. Everyone else happily chatted and drank rosé while getting their hair and nails done." Teagan snagged another one of the fritters. They weren't surprised when Margo and

George joined them, taking the container for themselves. "Anyway, she said the only argument happened between Cara and her brother Jimmy. They had quite the tiff outside the shop."

"About?"

"Apparently, Jimmy didn't approve of his younger sister marrying Valerie. She wasn't 'good enough' for Cara, in his words. It made for an awkward few minutes." Teagan grabbed one last banana fritter before going over to play with the dogs. "He tried to stop the wedding."

"Did he?" George spoke around the fritter he'd stuffed into his mouth. "Your auntie should give up hair and sell these. She'd be a billionaire."

"You can't sell love." Teagan grinned when Murphy laughed. "And yes, Jimmy Larkin made such a nuisance of himself, they barred him from the ceremony."

"The question is how far would Jimmy go if he thought he was protecting his sister." Murphy knew it wouldn't be the first time someone had killed for family. "It's a twisted motive, but murder often is."

FIVE

GEORGE

When Evan arrived ten minutes later, the container of banana fritters had been decimated. George had managed to get three of them for himself. It was a beautiful day, and being outside, he could almost forget what had happened.

Treacle and Bumble had happily found a play-mate in Teagan, who'd sat down in the grass with them. George returned to checking on the verbena and thyme. He was pleased with how they were doing; they'd managed to survive the last winter and hopefully would do well for another year.

One of the greatest joys of creating his wild-flower and bee-friendly garden was sitting in it with friends. He'd carefully curated the chaos. Whether

in the front or back of the cottage, he always wanted to feel as if he'd stepped through a portal into an ancient, magical place.

Evan's discovery of the banana fritters pulled his attention from where he'd been tending to a few unwelcome weeds. Or rather, his finding out they'd all been eaten. Murphy, of course, made sure to talk about how delicious they were.

"You couldn't have saved me one? Not even half of one?" Evan peered mournfully into the empty container. "A crumb of one?"

"No, no, we really couldn't have." Margo came over to join them. The dogs had finally tired themselves out and curled up together to enjoy the sun. "There's probably a few muffins left unless Captain Buzz and Paddington ate all of them already."

"There's plenty left. You gave me enough for an army. We've only eaten four of them." George shifted in his bee gear. He hadn't intended to stand around all morning in it, and it was starting to get uncomfortable. The fabric made him feel twitchy, but he put up with it for his bees. It wasn't ideal for hanging around in the garden with friends. "Why don't we go inside for tea? I don't want Bumble out in the cold for too long."

Leaving the others to follow, George whistled for Bumble. Both dogs led the way into the house with him close behind. He went into the back garden and pulled off his beekeeping suit, gloves, and hat, placing all of them in the shed before returning to the cottage.

Murphy was already in the kitchen, getting another round of coffee going. A wise decision on the whole. George grabbed the basket of muffins, carrying them into the living room. They'd all be far more comfortable there than in the kitchen.

It didn't take long to fill Evan in on his misadventure and the brief confrontation with the widow. Their solicitor friend covered his face with his hands, muttering curses to himself in several languages. George understood the general gist of it being about how frustrating they were as clients.

"Sarah's his cousin. He can't exactly tell her to bugger off." George didn't think she'd take it too well. The Bairds were a proud bunch—stubborn and prone to a bit of brooding. But they were also an incredibly close family. "We have to talk to her. Besides, it wasn't in an official capacity."

Evan chose to ignore all of them. Instead, he went over to Bumble and lifted him so they were nose to nose. "Now, young, furry lad. I want you to listen to me. No speaking to the police without your solicitor present. And remember, you can call me anytime, though the lack of opposable thumbs might be an issue."

"They said I wasn't a suspect. Margo has cameras." George gestured to his cousin, who was lounging on the sofa with Teagan. They made a cute couple. "You're all welcome to stay, but I've got to get into the garden and tend to my to-do list."

And he did.

But mostly, all the conversation and excitement from the past twenty-four hours had become overwhelming. George wanted to be alone with the plants and bees for a while. He grabbed his AirPods off the shelf behind the sofa and went outside.

They had been a gift from Murphy to replace his other headphones after Bumble had decided to see if they were tasty. They weren't, but they were also ruined. He often listened to music or podcasts while in the garden.

Shoving his earbuds in, George returned to the shed and donned his protective jacket and hat. He also picked up a few other items, including the entrance blocks. They'd help protect the hives against wasps during the rest of summer.

Bumble followed him partway down the garden

path towards the hives. But the pug abandoned him for the cottage and Treacle. He was always practically joined at the hip with the little Chihuahua.

Once at the hives, George set all his gear on the ground. He began a careful inspection of each one for Varroa. The aggravating mites could decimate an entire colony if not dealt with immediately.

To his relief, George didn't find a single one. He pulled his phone out of his pocket and did a short video about what to look for and how to take care of Varroa mites if they were found. It would be something he could edit into his next beekeeping video.

George filmed a second video, capturing all of the hives and how to install the entrance blocks. They were a critical line of defence against wasps. He didn't put them on every single entrance, just a few.

With both jobs complete across all of his hives, George walked around them for one last inspection. He checked the time on his phone and realised over two hours had flown by while he'd worked and filmed. His stomach complained loudly at not having taken a snack break.

After one final look, George replaced the lids on the hives. He gathered up his tools and retraced his steps to the cottage. It gave him time to check the new blackberry bushes and the wildflower patches on either side of the path.

They'd grown even taller over the past couple of months. He loved walking along this particular section of his garden. It was like being hidden in the fields out in the highlands; he'd brought a little bit of wildness into his home.

The organised chaos made him incredibly happy. Not everyone appreciated what he'd done. But the garden wasn't for them.

It was for him—and the bees.

Every single flower, herb, fruit, and everything in his garden was a pollinator. He'd done a massive amount of research into ensuring his garden was the most bee friendly and sustainable that it could be. And thus far, it seemed to be doing wonders for his hives.

"George?"

He pulled his AirPods out of his ears when he spotted Murphy at the top of the path. "Everything all right?"

"Heading into the brewery. Teagan and I have to check on our latest batch of blackberry mead. We used the blackberry honey you brought us a few months ago. We're doing a taste test of one of the bottles." Murphy waited for George to join him at the end of the path. "Margo's still here with the pups. Evan had to head to the office. He made sure to remind us of the importance of not speaking with the police without him."

"All right." George fidgeted with his earbuds, twisting them around in his fingers. He wondered if he should apologise for vanishing into the flora and fauna. "I'm going to work on the garden."

"Of course you are." Murphy placed a hand lightly on George's shoulder, giving it a comforting squeeze. "You've had quite the past twenty-four hours. Nothing wrong with needing to lose yourself in the garden. I'll be back later."

One thing George always appreciated about Murphy was how he never expected him to play neurotypical. He could just be himself. And sometimes, it meant he couldn't deal with people, even the ones he loved.

Following Murphy into the cottage, George veered off towards the kitchen while his boyfriend left for the brewery. Margo headed out as well, leaving him alone with a sleepy Bumble. He put the kettle on for tea and scrounged around for something to eat.

George peered into his freezer for far too long. He finally shook himself out of his thoughts. "What do you think, Bumble? Fancy leftovers?"

When he'd last visited, his dad had fixed up a few batches of his favourite potato curry. George grabbed one of the containers. It was easy to heat up in a pot on the stove, plus he could drop a couple naan into the toaster to go with it—comfort food at its finest.

For some reason, his parents, particularly his dad, were convinced he didn't eat sufficiently. Whenever they visited, they often wound up filling his freezer with meals. It was sweet and mildly amusing.

They'd taught him how to cook. He was decent enough at it and fully capable of remembering to eat. He'd learnt parents were going to parent no matter how old their children became.

Sitting outside with a bowl of curry and the naan, George contemplated the empty section of the garden. Bumble had found his favourite spot of shade underneath his chair. He was tempted to hold off on planting until after winter. Just because there was an empty spot in his garden didn't mean he had to fill it immediately.

After eating his curry, George decided to finish

trimming back the spring and summer growth in the front garden. It was one of the items left on his August to-do list. One of many things to accomplish in preparation for the descent into cooler weather.

It was a perfect late-summer day, with a gentle and cooling breeze and the bright sun overhead. George listened to the podcast of one of his fellow beekeepers while beginning to work. He had to nudge Bumble out of the way a few times.

George had gotten so lost in his trimming and the podcast that he didn't know anyone had approached until a hand touched his shoulder. He practically jumped out of his skin. "What the—"

"You were there."

"Pardon?" George sat back on his heels. He kept an eye on the woman who'd tapped him on the shoulder. "I don't know you."

"You were there." She had shoulder-length brown hair and a strong jaw. "You. Were. There."

George thought her tone might've been petulant or maybe sad. It was hard for him to tell. He didn't like being sat on the ground with her looming over him. "Please step back."

"You were there."

"Are you stuck on repeat?" George caught Bumble when he went to trundle towards the woman. He redirected him towards the other side of the garden. "Where was I? I'm not good with faces, but I think I'd remember you."

"You killed my wife." She started forward, and George fell backwards into the verbena to get out of the way. "I know you did."

"No, I didn't." George managed to extract himself from the verbena without crushing all of it. "She was most definitely dead when Bumble discovered her. There's a video to prove it."

"I—"

"Cara. What are you doing? The police told us to leave them alone." A man came up behind her. He caught her by the arms and drew her back from George. "I'm so sorry, mate. She's distraught. I'm Jimmy Larkin."

The man was clearly a relative. The two bore too much resemblance to not be siblings. George slowly got to his feet; he kept his shears in his hand but lowered towards the ground.

George didn't want to seem threatening, but she'd scared him for a moment. He reached up with his free hand to pull the earbud out of one ear. "George Sheth. This is my cottage. And my pug. He found the body while we were walking."

"The police mentioned that to us. Remember,

Cara?" Jimmy shook his sister as though trying to get her to listen. "I am so sorry. We're just so gutted about losing Val."

At the mention of her wife, Cara began wailing. It was an overly dramatic display. Something in Jimmy's expression made George wonder at how genuinely gutted the man was.

It felt off, but he couldn't pinpoint why. Expressions were always difficult for him to decipher. He kept a fair amount of distance between him and the siblings, not trusting either of them despite Jimmy seeming to believe the truth.

George didn't know what to say to either of them, particularly with Cara wailing. He didn't see any actual tears on her face. "I'm sorry for your loss?"

While George meant the words, they came out almost like a question. Was there a polite way to tell someone to go away? Jimmy finally decided to guide his wailing but not crying sister away towards a car parked up the lane.

George watched until the vehicle vanished from sight. He finally breathed a sigh of relief when it was gone. He bent down to pick Bumble up. "Why don't we have a calming mug of chai and a few biscuits?"

There was something about the Larkins that

bothered him. Neither of them had seemed sincere in their grief. Then again, he'd never been the best judge of other people's emotions.

He wished Murphy or Margo had been with him. They'd have been unable to assess the Larkins better. He couldn't stop thinking about the lack of tears.

Everyone grieved differently, but surely tears were involved when someone cried. George wondered if he should mention the visit to the police. They hadn't threatened him; it had been more disconcerting than anything else.

He had no doubts Sarah would be convinced he was investigating.

He wasn't.

Not yet, anyway.

"What do you reckon, Bumble?" George set him down in the kitchen. "Biscuits and tea to soothe the soul?"

Bumble immediately plopped down on his little bed in the kitchen, waiting patiently for his treat. George got the kettle going. He hunted in the cabinets for one of the chai blends his parents had brought back from their last trip.

"Tea, biscuits, and maybe I'll figure out why the

wailing confused me." George filled his little Loch Ness monster strainer with tea. He closed his eyes and listened to the water heating up in the kettle. It was one of his favourite sounds. "The wailing without tears."

SIX

MURPHY

MURPHY HAD SPENT MUCH OF THE AFTERNOON catching up on paperwork in his office. It was his least favourite part of running his own brewery and pub. His younger brother, Graeme, sometimes helped but was usually more of a hindrance, though his sister-in-law, Maisie, could be counted on to be of assistance.

While Murphy slaved over the books, Teagan had gone into the pub side of the building to give Maisie a hand with planning their next event. Since they only did tastings once a week, they could go all out. It was the area of the business where his sister-in-law thrived.

"Paddy?"

Murphy glanced up from his laptop, thankful for

the distraction. "Did Maisie and Graeme finally run you off with their madness?"

Teagan glowered at him. They had definitely endured enough time with his brother, who could test the patience of a saint. "We're supposed to be testing the blackberry."

"Why don't you grab the tester bottle? I'll finish these numbers. I'll be a minute or two." Murphy returned to the books. He added the last few receipts and closed his laptop, thankful to be finished. He went into the workroom to find Teagan already inspecting the mead. "How's it look?"

"We're absolutely buggered."

Murphy rushed over to inspect the bottle. "What's happened?"

"Give it a sniff." They practically shoved the tester into his nostril. "A whole sodding batch ruined. Bang goes Maisie's plans for the event next week. Our whole blackberry...."

"Are they all like this?"

"I'd wager every single one." Teagan cursed. They set the bottle on one of their worktables. "We've obviously buggered it up. What does the brewing book say about the recipe?"

Murphy took another sniff of the mead. The sharp sourness of vinegar smacked him in the face for a second time. "It's acetic. We're going to need to check the yeast strain we're using. Either it or the blackberries themselves may have introduced the bacteria."

Teagan went over to the shelf to grab their brewery journal. They kept details of every batch they'd ever made, starting back when Murphy had been brewing in his flat all alone. "Here we go. We've used the same yeast strain in our last three recipes. The previous two weren't disgustingly acetic."

"So, it's likely the berries." Murphy went into the dark room where they rested the meads. He took the larger jugs, carrying them into the room and setting them on the workbench. "George will be gutted. He'd really hoped to see what the blackberries would do in the mead with his blackberry honey."

"We can try again. We'll just be more careful with the blackberries." Teagan updated the journal with what had happened. "We've got the small batch of orange and saffron honey mead. It might be enough to cover the event, though I don't know if it'll fit her mystical, druidy theme."

"Druidy is not a word."

"Our mead is sodding vinegar. Druidy can be a word." Teagan finished with the journal and set it back on the shelf. "What are we going to do with this mess?"

"Dump it? Not salvageable." Murphy had experimented over the years with ways to fix bad batches of mead, but this wasn't going to work. "It's a waste."

With a sigh, the two picked up the bottles and emptied them. They'd be sterilised for use later. He tried to recycle when at all possible.

It was disappointing to see their hard work go down the drain. Murphy rarely had failures anymore. The first few years had involved a lot more trial and error. Now, they tended to have things running like a well-oiled machine.

"Cheer up, Paddy." Teagan gave him a few encouraging pats on the back. "We've got the orange and saffron mead. Plus, George brought us some of his chilli-spiced honey. We can work on a few new flavour combinations."

"What about a series of spiced chocolate meads?" Murphy carried the last of the bottles over to empty it out, then set it aside to be cleaned. "We could do a cherry and an orange."

"And a raspberry? Or maybe a caramelised honey and chocolate mead?" Teagan retrieved the journal. They flipped to a new page and began to jot down their ideas. "If we planned this out right, we could have a series of them right through autumn into winter."

"How much spiced honey do we have?"

"Enough for seven or eight medium-sized batches." Teagan dragged over one of the wheeled stools to sit on it. They set the journal on the table and bent forward. "We've got all those cocoa nibs, so we've got what we need to make a chocolate mead. The heat would be a nice addition, particularly since it'll be ready during the colder months. Nothing like a warm brew on a winter's night."

"Write that down. Maisie can use it in her next announcement." Murphy went over to the shelf to grab his personal recipe journal. He skimmed through the pages, hunting for one they could use as a base. "And we'll be extra careful with any of the fruit we use."

"Incoming."

Murphy looked up from the journal to find Teagan peering out through the window. "Oh?"

"A slightly frazzled Buzz and Bumble. I'll make tea. Looks like he could use it." Teagan darted over to open the door, waved at George, and returned to the little kitchen area of the brewery. They kept biscuits, tea, and coffee stocked. "If you're investigating, you have to let me go. I've got a wager going with Margo,

Evan, Graeme, and Maisie for when you get your-selves into trouble."

"Teagan, I love you, but please...." Murphy moved by them, going outside to meet George, who definitely seemed frazzled. Bumble panted happily from his arms, completely oblivious to his human's mood. "What happened?"

George shrugged. He carefully set Bumble on the ground, then shuffled forward to plant his fore-head against Murphy's chest. "People keep coming to the cottage."

"Oh? What people?"

"Maybe I could put up a Go Away sign?" George's voice was muffled by Murphy's shirt. "Big. Neon sign. Flashing lights. No, no lights. Those would annoy me. People annoy me."

Murphy pressed his lips together to keep from chuckling while he listened to George continue to list ways of keeping strangers away from his cottage. "A giant electric fence?"

"Too much?" George managed a laugh. He eased back from Murphy, gripping his arms. "I met Cara and Jimmy Larkin."

Murphy immediately frowned. He knew Elwin had told them to leave George alone. "What did they say?"

Guiding him into the brewery, Murphy wasn't surprised to see Teagan had set up three mugs for tea and a packet of biscuits. He glanced down to find Bumble pawing at his leg. The pug definitely knew exactly what he wanted.

Murphy chuckled. He walked over to his office, opened the door, and let Bumble meander inside to the plush bed on the floor by his desk. "Be a good lad for us."

Bumble circled the bed, pawed at the blanket for a second, and finally flopped down with a heavy sigh. Murphy laughed again before stepping out of the room. He turned to find George absently nibbling on a custard cream biscuit.

"Tea? Coffee? Hot chocolate?" Teagan lifted up the tin where they kept all the teabags and sachets of drink mixes. "We've got a little of everything."

"Oh." George reached blindly into the tin and picked one. "This'll do."

"Dark chocolate and raspberry hot chocolate? All right." Teagan grabbed the sachet and went over to their little coffee station. "Paddy?"

"Just a coffee."

Soon enough, the three of them were seated on stools around one of the worktables with their drinks and biscuits. George filled them in on his encounter with the Larkins. He seemed more bewildered than shaken by the experience.

"Why me?" George sipped the remnants of his hot chocolate. He'd gone through a number of biscuits as well. "Have I—"

Before George could continue, they heard a knock on the brewery door. Murphy exchanged a confused glance with Teagan, who went to answer. He followed them, with George twisting around on his chair to watch.

"Can we help you?" Teagan prompted when their visitor said nothing.

"I came to apologise."

Murphy stepped up closer. He opened the door wider to better look at the woman in front of them. She was mousey. Not just her brown hair and eyes but the timidity of her entire being. "To us?"

"To George. He's your boyfriend." Her statement sounded more like a question. "I'm Polly Collins. Valerie was my cousin. I wanted to apologise for Cara. She's very distraught, but it's no excuse to continually harass all of you."

Murphy glanced back at George, who nodded. They both knew this was a perfect opportunity to ask a few subtle questions of someone connected to the victim. Maybe they could get some inside information. "Why don't you come in? We were just sitting down with a cup of tea and biscuits. You're welcome to join us."

"Oh. Oh, I wouldn't want to impose." Polly hesitated. She shifted back and forth, offering an awkward smile before stepping into the brewery. "They mentioned in the village you all might be here."

Murphy raised an eyebrow at that. He wondered who she'd spoken with. "No secrets in a small village."

"No, I imagine not. It's very... quaint." Polly perched stiffly on the stool Teagan dragged over to join the others. They offered her a selection. "Just a plain tea. No milk, no sugar."

Interesting.

Murphy didn't know what to make of the soft-spoken woman. She wore a pale grey dress that hung limply on her body. It almost seemed as if she'd spent her life trying to disappear into the background, from her appearance to her mannerisms. "Did you know your cousin's new wife well?"

"Not very." Polly held a biscuit between the tips of her fingers, lifting it to her lips and lowering it without taking a bite. "Val and I didn't talk about her love life often. They had a whirlwind romance before deciding to marry. I talked her out of eloping. Family should be there."

"They were going to elope?" Teagan set a mug of tea in front of Polly.

"Yes." Polly nodded. She set the uneaten biscuit down and reached for the mug, which she held without drinking. "My auntie and uncle can be quite dramatic. They wanted to have a massive wedding for Val. But...."

"But?" Murphy encouraged her when she fell silent.

"But Cara's family wasn't so welcoming of Val." Polly finally sipped her tea. She set it down clumsily, sloshing liquid over the rim of the mug. "I should go. I'm supposed to help with the arrangements."

Before any of them could react, Polly raced from the brewery. Murphy grabbed a rag to clean up the mess. He dumped her mug in the sink, watching through the window as she fled down the lane. *How very, very odd.*

"Not sure I've ever met a more timid creature in my life." Teagan put away the tin of sachets and biscuits. They finished up their tea.

"That was odd, right? Not just me being me?" George snagged the last biscuit on the plate. He pried it apart to carefully eat the cream inside first.

"It was almost like she was afraid she'd said too much about the Larkins."

"Not just you. Definitely an odd bird." Murphy grabbed the empty dishes off the table and carried them over to the sink. He gave them a quick wash while Teagan filled George in on the failure of the blackberry mead.

His thoughts went back to the strange appearance of Polly Collins. Why had she decided to apologise for her cousin's in-laws? He couldn't make sense of the mousey woman who'd shrunk in on herself when they'd so much as glanced in her direction.

What exactly did the Larkins have to hide?

SEVEN
GEORGE

"Every single bottle?" George stared at the graveyard of broken mead dreams. He'd been excited to see what came from the honey he'd picked. "What a disaster. I hate this for you. All your effort gone to waste."

"Ah. We'll make a new batch. Come see the ideas we've had for your chilli-spiced honey." Teagan had obviously moved past their disappointment. "We're brainstorming. Want to give us a hand?"

Outside of his garden, the brewery was one of George's favourite places. He adored the creative energy when Teagan and Murphy plotted a new recipe. It was inspiring.

There was something almost stimulating about the atmosphere. It was clear to see how passionate they were about mead. They'd toss ideas back and forth while going through the collection of fruits, spices, and other ingredients at their disposal.

He sat on one of the stools, watching the two of them. They took small portions of the honey, mixing it with certain ingredients for a taste test. They were meticulous in wanting things to be perfect.

Who could blame them, given the results of the blackberry batch? He imagined they'd go above and beyond to try to prevent another mishap. It was like his hives; even if he did everything right, things could always go wrong.

"Here. Try this." Murphy stepped over with a spoon. He held it out to George. "What do you think?"

"Tastes like a spicy Jaffa cake." George licked the mixture off the spoon. He enjoyed the orange chocolate warmth coating his mouth. "Perfect. It'll be an amazing mead. You've got the flavours balanced perfectly."

While they went back to work on other recipe ideas, George went into the office to check on Bumble. His pug was snoring deeply, settled into the blankets in his bed. He went to sit on the floor and reached out to lightly scratch behind Bumble's ears.

It was calming. The office felt so much like

Murphy. George rested his head against the wall and closed his eyes, enjoying the hum of activity in the brewery and Bumble snuffling beside him.

"You okay?" Murphy came into the office several minutes later. He crouched in front of where George was sitting. "Why don't I take you home? We can have a quiet evening. There's the show you wanted to watch on Netflix. We can catch a few episodes together."

"Don't you have mead to make?"

"Not really. We've cleaned everything up. Teagan's got the bottles prepped to be sanitised. We've figured out our recipe. Nothing to do but wait until tomorrow morning to start the process. It's gone four now. Sent Tea to their auntie's. They'll see if there's any gossip about the wedding party for us." Murphy placed a hand on George's shoulder. "There's a two-for-one deal at the pizza place. We can grab a couple and have a lovely evening."

"Yeah?"

"Yeah. Pizza, beer, and just the two of us." Murphy hesitated when Bumble made a loud snort. "My apologies. Just the three of us."

George felt some of his remaining anxiety fade away. He had to laugh when Murphy engaged in a brief conversation with Bumble. "You get everything settled?"

"I have admitted my mistakes and promised to do better." Murphy winked at him. He rose to his feet and reached out his hand. "Ready to go?"

"I don't know. Floor's comfortable." George took the hand held out to him, letting Murphy help him get to his feet. "Well, maybe not that comfortable."

"The older you get, the less comfortable the floor becomes." Murphy led the way out of the office. "My words of wisdom for the day."

"Truly inspired." George snickered. He stretched his arms over his head, and they both laughed when his back audibly cracked. "Think I just proved your point."

The walk to the brewery had been nice, but George appreciated the ride back in Murphy's vehicle. Bumble had certainly already gotten his exercise for the day and then some. Poor old pug seemed ready for his dinner and his bed.

Since Murphy had called ahead, their pizzas were ready when they arrived. George's mouth started to water the second they were in the vehicle. They smelled absolutely divine.

"Heard a bit of choice gossip." Murphy slid back

into the driver's seat. "Seems Cara and Jimmy had a screaming match this afternoon."

"Oh? With each other?"

"Might as well have been. They were screeching at Polly." Murphy waved to someone who crossed in front of them and then began driving out of the village. "Tish at Pizza Palace said they were in the middle of the pavement saying all kinds of things about her. She simply stared at them without speaking a word."

"What were they saying?" George twisted slightly in the seat.

"Saying she tricked Val into signing a will excluding Cara." Murphy nodded when George gasped in surprise. "Tish said the Larkins seemed shocked. What if they assumed she was the beneficiary of her new wife's estate?"

"And Polly?"

"The little mouse claimed to have no idea she was the sole beneficiary." Murphy scratched his beard for a few seconds. "Not sure anyone believed her. It's an interesting twist to our murder mystery."

"Yes, what a twist, someone murdered a loved one over money." George hoped the past few months hadn't turned him into a complete cynic. "Am I being overly suspicious?"

"Given your experiences this summer? Probably not. I had the same thought," Murphy admitted. "I imagine we'll hear more about it from Teagan. Their auntie has likely heard every minute detail of the argument by this time."

They talked about mead and honey combinations for the rest of the short drive to his cottage. The divine smell of the pizza had his stomach grumbling loudly. George had to restrain himself from opening one of the boxes and grabbing a slice to eat in the vehicle.

Taking a couple drinks out of the fridge, George went into the garden. They set up some blankets near the firepit. Murphy had already gotten a fire going and propped up the laptop on a chair.

It was chilly enough to warrant a fire but not too cold to chase them inside. They got comfortable on the blanket, snuggled together with their pizzas, and Bumble curled up nearby. As the evening grew darker, George switched on all the faerie lights in the garden.

George was contemplating one last bite of pizza when their peaceful date night was shattered by shouting. "Not again."

"Let's go see what they want." Murphy picked up the two boxes of pizza, carrying them inside and setting them on the kitchen counter. "You might give the police a call. I'm fairly certain I recognise the dulcet tones of Cara Larkin."

"Again? For...." George dragged his fingers through his hair. He pulled a tie out of his pocket and gathered it up into a ponytail. "Why can't they leave me alone?"

"I don't know." Murphy frowned when someone pounded on the front door. "Call Elwin. Tell him that the widow can't seem to take his advice to leave you alone to heart."

"He's going to be annoyed."

"He'll be more annoyed if we don't call him." Murphy wasn't wrong.

While Murphy went to answer the door, George called Elwin on his cell phone. After a few rings, he answered and told them *not* to "engage with any of his potential suspects." The detective didn't seem to believe him when he claimed to not have wanted to speak to them in the first place.

George couldn't exactly deny it. But he hadn't wanted to see them at his cottage for what felt like a hundred times in the past week. "I'll be a good lad and stay inside."

"Paddy's already gone to speak with them, hasn't

he?" Elwin sighed heavily. "What am I going to do with the two of you?"

"Come rescue us from the distraught widow?" George hung up before Elwin said anything else. He hated speaking over the phone. Bumble trundled over to plop down on his foot. "Hello. Don't worry. Paddy's going to be fine, and so are we. We won't let the police arrest you for murder."

The joke lifted his spirits a little. George crouched down to give Bumble a scratch, then sent him off to his bed by the fireplace. He decided to listen to the conversation happening outside the cottage just in case Murphy needed his help.

All the shouting had stopped the second Murphy went outside. Inching closer to the door, George could hear raised voices. It mostly sounded like the Larkin siblings arguing with each other.

George cracked the door open after realising he hadn't heard Murphy speak. He found his boyfriend standing on the path while Jimmy and Cara were having a shouting match in the middle of the lane. It was a disturbingly familiar scene. "Paddy?"

Murphy glanced back at the cottage at the whisper. "Shut the door."

"I called Elwin."

"Brilliant. Shut the door before she sees you and changes the target of her aggravation." Murphy winked at him and then returned his attention to the Larkins. "I've never seen people so dedicated to shouting their problems out for the entire sodding county to hear."

"The volume's impressive." George winced when the raised voices went back to banshee-level shrieking. "What do they hope to gain?"

Murphy seemed to realise he wasn't going back inside, so he motioned for George to join him. "Cara has become hyper-focused on your knowing some secret. Don't ask me what or why, or how. I've no idea. Jimmy is concerned about her mental state and appears to show this by matching her volume in conversation."

"What is the point?"

"Not a single clue." Murphy shrugged. "Aside from ruining a perfectly lovely evening? I've no idea what they hoped to accomplish by this spectacle."

George leaned against him. He yawned noisily. "I'm bored. Is this what neurotypical siblings do?"

"I think it's what *they* do." Murphy nodded towards the siblings. He pointed down the lane where headlights could be seen. "I sense the arrival of the police."

George considered stepping behind Murphy to

hide. "Elwin might've told us to stay inside the cottage."

"Technically, we're on your property. We haven't left the garden." Murphy was unbothered by the impending lecture they were sure to receive. "Detective Inspector Smith likes to forget I've known him since we were both wee boys. I'm not intimidated by someone who used to eat dirt out of his ma's potted plants."

One of the local constables arrived first. He immediately went to separate the siblings. They thankfully stopped arguing with each other.

It was a few minutes before Elwin joined them. He spared a glance in their direction before going to have a hushed conversation with the siblings. In a surprisingly short amount of time, the Larkins were on their way, with the constable following after.

Elwin stalked up the lane towards them. He looked absolutely exhausted. "What happened to staying inside the cottage?"

"They were too busy shouting at each other to even notice me." George figured he'd been close enough that he could've bolted into the cottage if necessary. "Besides, I couldn't hear what was happening from inside."

"You couldn't...." Elwin pinched the bridge of his

nose and muttered under his breath for several seconds. "I'm not overly concerned with your hearing what's going on. I care about you staying safe."

"I was. They were over there." George pointed helpfully to where the Larkins had been arguing in the lane. "Not even close to me."

With an aggrieved sigh, Elwin threw his hands in the air. He stomped back down the path and over to his vehicle. George twisted his head to the side to hide his grin.

"Poor Elwin."

"Yes, I imagine it's always going to be difficult to be a detective inspector in the county where you were born." Murphy draped his arm across George's shoulders. "I know Sarah whinges about it often enough."

"Do you think Cara or Jimmy killed Valerie Collins?" George had learnt the hard way in the past few months that people often murdered the ones they claimed to love. "For whatever they believe was in the will?"

"I have no idea."

EIGHT

MURPHY

The evening hadn't been completely spoilt by the Larkins screaming themselves hoarse in the lane. Murphy lay awake, contemplating the murder mystery while George and Bumble snored in unison beside him. He had the former resting against his side while the latter had curled up between their pillows.

It was an adorable chorus of gentle snores. But Murphy couldn't sleep. He'd woken up a few hours after going to bed and now couldn't get his mind off the squabbling siblings.

Why was Cara Larkin so hyper-focused on George? The detectives had repeatedly told her of his innocence. They'd even gone so far as to show her the video from Margo's cottage.

There was no way George could be involved in the murder. So why couldn't the woman let it go? There had to be something they were missing. On the other hand, Jimmy Larkin did seem to grasp George's innocence.

The argument in front of the cottage had consisted mainly of Jimmy telling his sister to let it go and Cara insisting they had to prove what happened to Valerie. It hadn't offered much insight to Murphy. But he couldn't get one thing out of his mind. When Murphy had stepped outside, Jimmy had been admonishing her to wait it out.

Wait it out?

Wait what out?

The phrase plagued him so much he couldn't sleep. What had Jimmy wanted her to wait out? The murder inquiry? Or the will? He hadn't heard what Cara responded; it was one of the few moments when she hadn't been exercising the full range of her vocal ability.

A sudden bark from Bumble caught his attention. The pug had jolted up and rushed to the edge of the bed. He went around in a circle and then pawed at it repeatedly.

Bumble rarely barked. Very rarely. Murphy sat up, setting the pug on the floor. He got out of bed and dragged on the T-shirt that he'd tossed on a chair before going to sleep.

"Come on, old man. Let's see what spooked you." Murphy followed Bumble out of the bedroom. He'd expected the pug to want into the back garden; instead, he went towards the front door. "What's—"

A barely audible tap caught his attention. Murphy frowned. Had someone knocked on the door?

Pausing for a moment to listen before continuing, Murphy inched towards the door. He tried to keep Bumble behind him, but the recalcitrant pug didn't want to listen. The tapping became full-out knocking.

"It is just after five in the morning." Murphy yanked the door open, fully expecting to see one of the Larkins. "Polly?"

"I think they're trying to kill me." Polly stumbled forward into his arms.

Murphy had to lunge forward to grasp her. He managed to keep her on her feet and dragged her into the cottage. "Who's trying to kill you?"

"They're trying to kill me to get the money." Polly shook uncontrollably. She dropped onto the couch and buried her face in her hands. "They're trying to kill me."

While Polly kept repeating herself, Murphy grabbed his phone. He sent a text message to both Elwin and Sarah. If he had to speak with another hysterical person, so did they.

They were paid to contend with the families of murder victims. He wasn't. It was too early in the morning to deal with her.

"I'll make you some tea." Murphy raised an eyebrow at her teary-sounding "Okay" but went to turn on the kettle. He hadn't actually seen any moisture in her eyes. Bumble bumped his head into his leg to get his attention. "Are you wanting a little walk in the garden?"

With Bumble in the garden, Murphy went into the kitchen to make good on his promise of tea. George joined him a few minutes later. His long hair was an absolute mess, and he had the duvet wrapped around him like fabric armour.

"Why is she here?" George kept his voice down.

"She thinks Cara and Jimmy want to kill her." Murphy opened the cupboard to retrieve multiple mugs. He had no doubts Elwin and maybe Sarah would be joining them as well. "It's all she kept saying when I opened the door."

"I have heard and even comprehended the words coming out of your mouth. But I still don't actually understand. Why is she here? What are we supposed to do?" George shuffled closer to him, stumbling a little over the edge of the duvet. "We're not the police or armed or anything likely to be useful if someone is trying to do her in."

"You're not wrong." Murphy kept an eye on Polly, who continued to tremble and quietly sob into her hands. "Maybe she decided we were on her side?"

"We've seen her a grand total of one time." George dropped into one of the kitchen chairs. "Have you texted Elwin or Sarah?"

"I have."

"Brilliant. Did you call Evan?" George stretched his arm out and grabbed his noise-cancelling earbuds from the kitchen counter. "He'll be cross if we don't keep him updated on what's happening."

"We'll wait until it's not a completely ridiculous hour."

"Is she getting snot and tears on my pillow?" George peered into the living room. He blinked blearily at Murphy, who couldn't help a quiet chuckle. "What?"

"Not sure I actually saw tears." Murphy grabbed his phone off the counter when it buzzed. "Elwin's on his way. He decided not to send constables.

Sarah's threatened to throw both of us in jail for an indeterminate amount of time for waking her up."

"Let's not mention the threat to Evan. She is joking, right?"

"Probably." Murphy patted George's shoulder and adjusted his duvet for him. "Why don't you go back to sleep?"

"And miss the story behind this?" George gestured to the sniffling woman in the living room. "Can we stop whispering?"

"Only if you want to stop talking about her." Murphy grabbed his collection of tea strainers and the tin of loose-leaf tea. "It's strange that she came all the way here from the village. Not a massive drive or even a walk, but she's staying at the bed and breakfast. Why not ask Sky or Brannon to call the police?"

"Or call them herself?"

"Why make the journey all the way out to your cottage?" Murphy lowered his voice even further when they heard her make an extra noisy sniffle. George shuddered. "I'll take her some tissue."

"And tea."

"Tea and tissues." Murphy grinned when George rolled his eyes. "Bumble appears to be done in the garden."

"I'll grab him and go put on something other

than shorts and a duvet."

After brushing a kiss to George's lips, Murphy grabbed the kettle when it finally finished boiling. He poured water into each mug, amusing himself with the multiple bobbing Loch Ness monsters. The tea strainers were his favourite out of his boyfriend's large collection.

Everyone always seemed to buy him new ones. He had an entire drawer in the kitchen to house them. They all got used, but the Loch Ness monster strainers tended to be everyone's favourite.

Once a few minutes had passed, Murphy carried one of the mugs into the living room. He set it on the coffee table in front of Polly. She sniffled repeatedly before finally uncurling herself enough to reach for it.

"Thank you."

Murphy grabbed his own cup and sat on the arm of the sofa. "Do you want to talk about it?"

"You won't believe me."

"You won't know until you try. You haven't really said much. I can't say whether or not I believe you. Why don't you tell me what's happened?" Murphy knew the detective inspectors would be annoyed, but his curiosity got the better of him. "What makes you think they want to kill you?"

"They moved out of the bed and breakfast."

"Right." Murphy schooled his features not to show absolute disbelief. "Are they headed back home, then?"

"No, they've rented an Airbnb outside your village." Polly clutched the mug in both of her hands as if trying to warm herself. "I heard them whispering about dumping me."

"Dumping you?" Murphy didn't think it necessarily meant they were trying to kill her. Maybe in context with how her cousin Valerie had died and been left in the lane, it might be enough to make a person with a nervous disposition more suspicious. "Did they say anything else?"

"I couldn't hear." Polly had kept her gaze on the mug the entire time. He tried not to judge since she'd experienced a traumatic event, and a lack of eye contact didn't really mean anything. "They keep telling me that we should all head home together."

"Okay." Murphy didn't want to be dismissive; she might stop talking to him. "Did you drive to Dufftown together?"

"Well, yes." Polly shifted. She flinched when George returned. He'd gone for comfortable clothing —jeans and a long-sleeve T-shirt. "What did you see?"

"Pardon?" George paused in his attempt to straighten out one of his sleeves. "What did I see when?"

"When you found poor Val."

"Ah. Not much." George shrugged. He yanked on his sleeve a few more times. "Once I realised what Bumble had stumbled on and knew she was beyond my help, I kept my distance."

"But did you see them? Did you see Jimmy and Cara? I know they did this. I know it." Polly had shifted her gaze directly on George, who Murphy could see was growing increasingly uncomfortable with the fervour in her voice. "What did you see?"

The uncomfortable moment was interrupted by a loud knock on the door. Murphy wasn't surprised when George bolted to answer it. Polly's questions had clearly unnerved him.

"Detective Inspector Smith." Murphy nodded to Elwin, who'd thankfully arrived fairly promptly. He lifted his mug of tea. "Fancy a cuppa?"

"No." Elwin gave a resigned sigh. "Ms Collins? Why don't you come with me?"

"They're going to kill me."

Elwin glanced from Polly over to Murphy, who shrugged. "I'm Detective Inspector Smith. We've met. I'm not sure if you remember. I'm not going to let anyone hurt you. Why don't you come back to the station with me? We can talk about why you think someone is trying to kill you."

His calm approach did wonders with Polly. She finally nodded and set her mug of tea down. Elwin sent a withering glare at Murphy before guiding her out of the cottage.

"Right." Murphy scrubbed his hands over his face. He wanted nothing more than to go back to bed, but it was almost six. "Not much point in going back to sleep. Why don't we walk into the village for breakfast? Café opens around six. We could pop by to see if Margo wants to join us."

George lounged on the sofa, blinking tiredly at Murphy. "I'm trying to figure out what on earth she thought we could do to help."

"Not sure I even want to make a guess." Murphy slumped down onto the couch beside him. George immediately leaned into him with a tired sigh. "We could skip breakfast."

"Most important meal of the day—or so Mum drilled into me for the entirety of my childhood. A walk and coffee might perk me up for the rest of the day." George stared down at his sleeve. "I think I put my shirt on inside out."

Murphy reached over to touch the stitching

visible along the seam. "You definitely put your shirt on inside out."

"It was weird, right?"

"What? Your shirt?"

"No." George swatted him lightly on the chest. He sat up and ripped off his shirt before putting it on the right way. "Her questions for me. The way she kept asking if I'd seen anything. It was odd. It felt... odd."

"It wouldn't be out of the ordinary to wonder if you'd seen the killer or killers."

"True." George didn't sound convinced. "There's something not quite right about her."

"I think there's something not quite right about everyone connected to this murder." Murphy yawned widely. He ran his fingers through his beard. "Let's head into the village for breakfast. I'm eager to see if there's any gossip."

"Fine."

"And George? It's not just you. Something's definitely odd about all of them—including Polly." Murphy pushed himself to his feet. He glanced down at his bare feet. "I should probably get fully dressed first."

NINE

GEORGE

After a quick whizz around the garden to check on his flora and buzzy bees, George had led the walk down the lane to Margo's. His cousin was already out in her front garden, doing some weeding while Treacle inspected every blade of grass. She'd waved off the invitation for breakfast, though Bumble had wandered over to flop beside his best friend.

"Leave him if you want. I'll be out here most of the morning." Margo made them promise to stop by later to give her all the gossip about what had happened. "You might have a chat with Alyssa at the café. Her girlfriend owns the Airbnb where Jimmy and Cara went to hide out."

Saying their goodbyes, George wasn't surprised

when Bumble eyed them for a second before deciding to stay on the grass. They walked down the lane without their trundling little pug. Murphy stopped near where Valerie's body had been found.

"Paddy?"

Murphy walked slowly along the right side of the lane. "She wasn't killed here."

"Right." George moved over to stand beside him. He gestured towards where the body had been. "It had to have been dumped. There'd have been blood otherwise."

"Maybe. They said they didn't believe she'd been killed here. But what if she was murdered close by? Hit over the head? Maybe she stumbled down the lane before collapsing here." Murphy scratched at his jaw absently, running his fingers through his beard. "Elwin mentioned Valerie died from blunt force trauma. That could mean anything from a rock to hitting your head on the ground."

"It also makes me think it wasn't planned."

"We've both seen how emotionally trigger-happy the Larkins are." Murphy said what George had been thinking. Both Jimmy and Cara seemed impulsive and volatile. "Why don't you take this side, and I'll walk the other? Maybe we'll see something the police didn't on our trek into the village."

Given days had passed, George wasn't expecting to find anything. The police had searched the area. Though he didn't know how far down the lane they'd gone.

It made more sense for a fatally injured Valerie to have stumbled down the lane than for her to be randomly dumped out of a vehicle. If the killer had placed her intentionally, wouldn't they have picked somewhere else? They'd surely have wanted to find a more secluded spot.

Not the middle of the lane.

Had the killer watched until they were certain Valerie wouldn't get back up?

It was a terrifyingly sad thought. George was about to call out to Murphy, whose longer legs had carried him further down the lane, when he spotted an oddly damaged bit of hedge. He inched closer.

"Paddy?" George crouched down to inspect the hedge. "Does this look as if someone's fallen on it and rolled around?"

Murphy strode back towards him. He came over to get a closer look. "Something fell on it. Not sure what."

"There's stones from the wall a little further up the lane. Maybe the killer grabbed one? Valerie walked in front of them. They might've argued."

George stood up. He used his phone to take a few photos, glancing around to see if anything else stood out. "I don't see a potential murder weapon."

"Might've taken it with them or dumped it when they ran." Murphy suggested he send the video to Elwin. "Let's continue on. Maybe we'll see something the killer threw."

"It'd be impossible to prove, I suppose. There's no blood anywhere on the hedge, but I don't remember it being flat." George continued on his side of the lane. He didn't see the "smoking gun" of a bloody rock. It was likely too much to hope for them to have one of those movie mystery moments where the weapon suddenly appeared. "I wonder if Sky and Brannon made breakfast."

While Murphy messaged the bed and breakfast owners, George continued his inspection along the side of the lane. Elwin had responded to the video, saying the police were aware of the hedge. His text also included a strongly worded request to stop hunting for trouble.

It was a little unfair. George hadn't been searching for trouble when it had banged on his door multiple times in the past few days. It felt as though it would find him no matter what he tried.

Hiding away in the cottage hadn't helped. He'd

done everything in his power to avoid anyone connected to Valerie Collins. They still appeared to be quite invested in dragging him into the police investigation despite his best intentions.

To his mind, George thought being proactive was better than waiting for the inevitable. Maybe if they unmasked the killer, random strangers would stop invading his peace and quiet. He hoped.

"Sky said to pop on by. They've got a full breakfast this morning and no one to enjoy it because their guests are all suspiciously absent." Murphy pocketed his phone. He crossed the lane to walk beside George. "Anything from Elwin?"

"They were aware of the hedge. He wouldn't give me anything else aside from telling us to mind our own business." George kept his eyes on the ground, searching for any signs of the murder. He wondered how far the police had gone in their own investigation. "Think Elwin walked all the way to the village?"

"Probably. Or at least where the lane connects with the next street." Murphy went back over to the other side to continue looking. "I wonder how far someone could walk after being bashed in the head."

"No idea—and I'm not searching on Google. I

don't want them thinking I did something." George didn't care if he was being overly paranoid. Experience had taught him being innocent didn't necessarily guarantee anything in a criminal inquiry. "From movies and the telly, they make it seem like someone either collapses immediately or can crawl a small distance."

"I imagine the truth depends on how hard the person was hit."

"True." George didn't believe they'd find anything. He still kept his gaze firmly on the grass and hedge on his side of the lane. "What if Valerie were struck more than once?"

"Elwin's not going to tell us. He got in trouble for what he told us last time." Murphy suddenly stopped, crouching down to inspect something in the grass. "Check this out."

George jogged across the lane. It took a moment before he spotted the glinting silver almost completely hidden in the grass. "Don't touch it."

"Not planning on it. I'll take a photo and send it to Elwin. So he can yell at me and not you this time." Murphy had his phone out and snapped a couple of images. "Looks like a heart with a C and V in the centre."

"Cara and Valerie?" George hazarded a guess.

"Chain of the necklace is broken. Think it was snapped?"

"Maybe the killer yanked it off in the process of the murder?" Murphy's phone buzzed in his hand before George could respond. "Elwin's on his way. He said not to touch anything. There's also a quite creative string of swear words. I'm impressed. I didn't think he had it in him."

Deciding to continue on down the lane a little, George searched for any other signs of the victim or killing. It would likely be impossible to tell if the flattened grass was from the day of the murder or came after. He didn't find any blood spatter or a stray rock.

"The killer had to take the weapon with them. Maybe they dumped it elsewhere. But I'm not seeing anything else." George checked both sides of the lane but didn't find any other signs of the murder. "Do you think the attack happened on the lane?"

"Maybe. There's also the possibility of rain having washed away any blood." Murphy had a good point since they'd gotten a brief storm not long after the murder. "I'm surprised they didn't find the necklace."

"Elwin's going to be thrilled we found it."

Elwin was, in fact, not thrilled when he arrived ten minutes later. He stomped around like a bear with a wounded paw while taking photos and carefully gathering the evidence. With barely a nod of acknowledgement, he got back in his vehicle and drove off.

"Not sure we're getting a Christmas card this year." Murphy winked at George, who chuckled. "All right. We better hurry before Brannon decides we don't want breakfast. I'd hate to have to raid their kitchen."

George eyed him suspiciously for a moment. "Joke."

"Correct. I'd greatly enjoy raiding his kitchen." Murphy stepped back onto the lane. "Might as well keep an eye out."

While they headed into the village, George's mind was only partially focused on continuing their hunt for clues. He couldn't stop thinking about the necklace. His mind went over a variety of scenarios on how it wound up hidden on the side of the lane.

Had it been accidentally ripped off in the struggle and thrown to the side? Or maybe the victim had done it to leave a trail. George hadn't seen any blood on it, but it had rained.

He turned his mind to their three potential suspects—Polly, Cara, and Jimmy. It was unlikely the killer had been a stranger. All three seemed to have at least some semblance of a motive.

"Shilling for your thoughts?"

"Hmm?" George stumbled over a dip in the lane. He caught himself before he tumbled to the ground. "Sorry. Did you say something?"

"You seem deep in thought."

"Polly, Cara, and Jimmy."

"Our trifecta of potentially disturbed suspects?" Murphy paused to look at something under a hedge but seemed to dismiss it. "What about them?"

"Who do you think killed Valerie?" George hadn't made his mind up yet. "I can't get away from Cara and Jimmy's behaviour."

"Maybe they were all involved." Murphy grabbed George's arm to pull him back when a car went flying past. "Remind me to text Elwin that his cousin seems to think he's driving in the Grand Prix."

"Poor teenager." George slipped his hand into Murphy's as they ventured across the lane to the street leading into the village.

It was a beautiful morning. They enjoyed the rest of their walk to Sky and Brannon's. They hadn't found anything else incriminating, but the necklace had been provocative enough.

"Hello." Sky was cleaning the front windows of their bed and breakfast. She gave a cheerful wave as they made their way up the path. "Can you believe they all fled before five in the morning? I made breakfast and went upstairs to wake them up as requested only to find them gone."

"Who? I thought the Larkins had already left for an Airbnb?" Murphy thankfully took up the conversation. George needed more coffee before he was ready to engage in more than a somewhat polite grunt of greeting. "Did you see any of them the night of the murder?"

Sky stopped scrubbing at a spot on the window. "We went to bed early that night. I couldn't tell you."

"How many of the guests did you have staying?"

"We had six of the wedding guests, including Polly." Sky had an odd tone to her voice that George couldn't quite decipher. "The still-living bride and her brother fled yesterday after a massive row with her. The rest of the Larkins' friends and family vanished this morning. No idea where or why. I'm glad we insist on payment in advance."

"What's wrong with Polly?" Murphy had obviously picked up on Sky's tone as well.

"She's... strange."

"Strange how?" George asked when no one else

spoke. "They've all been a little odd. Everyone's a little odd."

"I thought at first she was just a shy creature. Nothing wrong with that, of course. But she spent an awful lot of time on the phone since the murder. She had a meeting with some solicitor yesterday as well." Sky finished cleaning the front door and opened it for them. "The row she had with the Larkins. For a small mouse of a woman, she had quite a roar to her."

"Did she?" Murphy exchanged a glance with George. Polly Collins clearly had more depth to her than they'd seen. "Did Cara or Jimmy threaten her? She was around our place in the early hours of the morning claiming they wanted to kill her."

George tried not to grin like a fool at Murphy calling the cottage "our place." "She was convinced they had plans for her."

"I never heard a threat." Sky shrugged. "I didn't eavesdrop on the entire conversation. They mostly argued about who got Valerie's money and jewellery. She apparently inherited quite a collection from her grandmother."

"Jewellery?"

"Yeah, nattered on about masses of jewellery Valerie had inherited from her nan." Sky nodded towards the little dining room. "Go on. I'll bring you some coffee and toast to go with your breakfast."

George followed Murphy into the dining room. He didn't know what to make of Polly. "Maybe coffee will help this all make sense."

"It can't hurt."

TEN
MURPHY

"Jewellery."

"Makes you wonder." Murphy thought about texting Elwin to see if he was aware of the conversation. He decided to wait since their detective inspector friend had seemed rather annoyed with them. "Just because we found a necklace doesn't mean it's connected."

"True." George grabbed one of the rashers of bacon and took a bite. He waved it around, gesturing towards the stairs leading up to where the rooms were. "Think they might've left anything behind?"

"I doubt it. We could always ask." Murphy knew Brannon would probably let them peek into the bedrooms. "They're usually on top of cleaning after a guest leaves."

"Even ones who duck out in the middle of the night?" George had an excellent point. "Elwin's never going to forgive us for sticking our noses into another investigation."

"He'll live."

They finished up their breakfast. Brannon joined them towards the end, topping up their coffees and making a sandwich for himself from some of the leftovers. Murphy bided his time and waited for a good moment to ask a few questions.

"Go on, then." Brannon had obviously grown tired of waiting. "I can see you want to ask something. Playing DI again, are we?"

"Not exactly," George muttered defensively.

"Did you notice anything strange about your disappearing guests?" Murphy stirred sugar into his coffee before taking a sip. Brannon made his brew as strong as the sludge his granddad used to drink in the mornings. "Maybe they left something behind?"

"Not a thing. Not even in the rubbish. I was stripping sheets off the beds before I made breakfast. No stray sock. Nothing in the bins. That's probably the strangest part of it all." Brannon dragged a spare chair from another table to sit beside them. "There's always a random tissue or bit of paper. I've never had a guest take their trash with them."

"Did you hear about the wedding?" Sky came over to stand behind her husband. She rested her hands on his shoulders. "Jimmy. The brother? He had a massive argument right before the ceremony, trying to talk his sister out of marrying Valerie."

"We did." Murphy wondered if there was more to the motive than monetary gain. "What did you hear? Was there a particular reason?"

"My baby sister was there. She said he went on about Valerie not being good enough for Cara." Sky shrugged indifferently. "They didn't seem to like the cousin either. Polly? Quiet as a mouse. Never said a peep to me aside from an awkward hello."

Polly.

Murphy didn't know what to make of Polly. "She's an interesting one."

"Followed her cousin around like a lost little duck, constantly by her side. Valerie treated her like her personal assistant. She barked orders at Polly. It was... sad and strange." Sky shook her head. She stretched her arm out to snag one of the remaining bits of bacon on the table. "Hungry for anything else, or can I start clearing things up? And don't be trying to pay us. Since our guests ran off on us, this would've all gone to waste without someone to eat."

No matter how Murphy tried to protest, they

refused to let him pay for breakfast. He hadn't intended to grab a free meal. Sky waved off his offer and wandered off with a stack of plates in her arms.

George had been quiet throughout the conversation. He glanced over at Murphy when they were alone. "We could take a walk."

"Anywhere in particular you want to go?" Murphy thought he had a good idea of where. "Maybe go ask a couple of siblings if they recognise a necklace?"

"No harm in asking a few questions." George stuffed the last piece of bacon into his mouth.

"You choke that down, and we'll go. Maybe we can learn something along the way when we walk through the village." Murphy chugged down the last of his coffee. He set his mug down as Brannon came back over to them. "Something wrong?"

"The oddest thing."

"Yes?" Murphy prompted when their friend didn't elaborate. "What's the oddest thing?"

"I went back into Cara Larkin's room. I swear on my life I emptied the rubbish—I do all of them together so I don't forget one." Brannon lifted up the small bin in his hand. "There's a crumpled wedding invitation with blood on it."

"Don't touch it." Murphy grabbed Brannon's

wrist when he went to reach in for the paper. "Give Sarah or Elwin a call to tell them about it. But... maybe don't mention us. We should go."

"Still driving the poor detective inspectors to distraction?" Brannon set the bin on the floor. He nodded towards the door. "Off with you. I won't mention you were asking all sorts of probing questions about our guests. I'll even tell you what they say if they come to pick this up."

Making a quick escape, Murphy and George strode away from the bed and breakfast. Murphy eyed the gathering clouds in the distance, hoping it wasn't an ominous sign for the rest of the day. Rain would be inconvenient, if nothing else, since they'd decided to walk.

Murphy draped his arm around George's shoulders. "What do you think?"

"Teagan has news for us."

"What?" Murphy frowned in confusion until he realised they were coming down the lane towards them. "Morning, Tea. What's got you up so early?"

"Work? You know, the thing you pay me to do?" Teagan had a croissant in one hand and a large thermos in the other. "What are *you* doing? Shouldn't you be at the brewery?"

"We're—"

"Investigating the murder despite Elwin's empty threats." Teagan grinned before taking a massive bite of their croissant. "Oh, my auntie had a bit of gossip for you."

"Come on. Walk with us. We're exploring the village." Murphy started walking again.

Teagan shrugged before falling into step with them. "My auntie heard from one of her regular clients, whose son owns the café. They mentioned how Cara made threats to Valerie before the wedding. Our poor victim had second thoughts about getting married."

"Interesting. What was the threat?" George asked.

"Not a clue. Take all of it with a massive grain of salt. This particular gossip source isn't always the most reliable." Teagan had another bite of their croissant before continuing, "They also claimed you were in love with your sister-in-law."

Murphy tripped over his feet and stumbled forward, almost dragging George to the ground in the process. "I'm sorry. What?"

"I did say they weren't reliable." Teagan snickered while Murphy heaved a dramatic sigh. "Apologies. While I picked up my breakfast, I also heard that the little group of wedding guests at

Dahlia's Airbnb had a massive argument this morning."

"Oh?" Murphy forgave them immediately over his own curiosity. "About?"

"I'm sure we can find out since you're obviously walking towards her Airbnb." Teagan continued grinning at him while finishing the croissant.

"I've not known anyone who could eat with an air of smugness like you." Murphy rolled his eyes when Teagan clearly took it as a compliment.

The trio made their way down one lane into the next. They wound up stopping to say good morning to a few friends. Murphy confirmed the upcoming dates for events at the brewery when they asked; he could see George growing increasingly fidgety the further they were delayed.

They eventually made it to the street with Dahlia's cottage. It was a decent-sized home with multiple rooms. Murphy had been inside many times as a boy.

"Now what?" Teagan had moved on to their thermos of coffee. "We can't exactly knock on the door. What are we going to say? Got a Hoover for sale?"

"We didn't think this far ahead." Murphy slowed

his steps to a more meandering pace. "Maybe we'll get lucky."

To his utter amazement, they did get lucky. Cara and Jimmy were outside the cottage. They appeared to be packing up their things. It was odd, considering they'd just moved from the bed and breakfast.

Were they fleeing the village?

Or maybe even the country?

"Morning." Teagan gave a cheery wave before Murphy could stop them. "Leaving for home?"

"You."

Before anyone could say anything, Cara launched herself at George. She had a hand on his throat and clawed at his face. He managed to kick her back, allowing Jimmy to rush forward and grab his sister.

Murphy caught George by the arms and yanked him out of reach of the flailing woman. "Are you all right? Take a breath."

"I'm fine," George wheezed after a moment. He tried to wave off Murphy's concern, but he could see the slight tremble of his hand. "I'm fine. I'm fine. Just give me a second."

The more George repeated he was fine, the less Murphy believed him. He knew drawing attention to it would make things worse. It would be better to allow him a moment without everyone hovering.

"This is why I'm trying to get her out of the village," Jimmy snapped. He'd handed his sister off to a couple of people who'd come out of the cottage. "Is he okay?"

Murphy stepped in front of George, blocking him from view. "He'll be fine. So you're leaving?"

"We are." Jimmy folded his arms across his chest. He glowered defiantly. "What of it?"

"Are the police aware?"

"None of their business." Jimmy took a single step forward, then backed down when Murphy didn't budge. "All of this is too much for my sister. She's... delicate."

Delicate?

Of all the words to describe Cara Larkin, that was definitely not at the top of the list. Teagan seemed to be as amused as he was by the description. They had their phone in hand; he wondered if they were recording the conversation.

When Constables Natalie Bettley and Sean Davie strolled down the lane towards them a few minutes later, Murphy understood immediately what Teagan had done. They'd texted the police.

They knew each other well enough for them to send a quick message about the assault.

"Is this really necessary?" Jimmy tried to stop the constables from reaching the cottage where Cara had retreated. "Honestly. It was a simple misunderstanding."

"A misunderstanding? She grabbed him by the throat. Not sure you can misconstrue it as anything other than assault." Murphy had been trying to keep his temper, but the casual dismissal of what was now the third attempt by Cara Larkin to do harm sent him off. "It's absolutely necessary. You absolute—"

"Paddy. Why don't you lot head back into the village? Maybe have some tea. Calm yourself down." Sean immediately stepped between Murphy and Jimmy. "Go on. We'll come speak with you when we're finished here."

Murphy hesitated briefly. He trusted Sean and Natalie, but something had to be done. "She's going to wind up killing someone."

"Let us do our jobs. Please, Paddy," Sean implored. He put his hands up and walked Murphy back a few steps. "I promise we're not going to let anyone get away with assault."

"Paddy?" George came up behind him. He

placed a hand on Murphy's shoulder. "Come on. I could use some tea."

The journey back went far quicker than their casual walk to the Airbnb. Murphy insisted on stopping at the clinic to make sure George was okay. His boyfriend didn't appreciate the fuss, but it seemed wise.

Aside from a few scratches and a bruise, George had come out of his encounter with Cara unscathed. The doctor was happy for him to go. They left the clinic and intended to make their way to the café, but Detective Inspector Smith caught up with them.

"Why is it always you three?" He pulled up beside them in his vehicle and got out. "Honestly. You can't possibly expect me to believe you randomly found yourselves walking by the cottage they'd rented."

"I mean, we could technically expect you to believe it." George definitely seemed more than ready to be far away from people. "Technically. Very technically."

"George." Elwin pinched the bridge of his nose. He shook his head a few times before clearing his throat loudly. "Are you okay? Were you hurt?"

"Few scratches." George tilted his head back to

show the slight damage. "I'm fine. I don't understand why she... I don't understand why."

"We've brought her in for questioning. We plan on, if nothing else, following up on common assault charges. If it's a first offence, I imagine she'll get away with a fine." Elwin checked his phone when it buzzed. "Try to stay out of this inquiry? Please. The last thing I want is anyone else being hurt."

"We'll do our best," Murphy promised.

"Somehow, I am not relieved." Elwin looked at each of them momentarily before shaking his head again. "I suppose it's the most I can ask."

"Did you find anything at Sky and Brannon's?" Murphy asked when Elwin went to leave. "The bloody paper in the bin?"

"How did you—you know what, I don't want to know."

"You have in the past." Murphy was immune to the glare Elwin sent his way. "All right, all right. I apologise. We'll try to keep ourselves clear of the inquiry."

"You're a fibber, but I appreciate the sentiment."

ELEVEN

GEORGE

THE CAFÉ WASN'T PACKED, BUT EVEN THE handful of people overwhelmed him. George wanted tea and quiet. Murphy, thankfully, knew him well enough to read between the lines.

His shock hadn't quite worn off yet. George stayed outside the café with Teagan. They were a quiet sentry at his side, deflecting anyone who might want to stop for a chat.

No one did.

George wondered if he was giving off a "leave me alone" air. Murphy joined them with three cups in his hands. He grabbed one while Teagan took the second. "Thanks."

"Why don't we head to the brewery? It's closer than your cottage." Murphy led the way down the lane. "We can have a quiet chat. Maybe see if Margo wants to join us with the pups."

With a slight nod, George focused on his tea and not tripping. He'd had enough excitement for one morning. Their lovely breakfast sat heavy in his stomach.

Taking a slow sip of tea, George had to smile in relief. Murphy had gotten him a lemon ginger blend with what tasted like a healthy dollop of honey. It would do wonders for his stomach and his nerves.

They walked so slowly that it took almost twice as long as it usually would've. George needed the extra time. Margo was already there when they reached the brewery; she had a basket in one hand with Treacle and Bumble dancing around her feet.

George was growing increasingly anxious. He wanted everything to stop, even his friends' quiet chattering. "I'm going home."

"George?" Murphy was immediately concerned. He set his tea down and came closer. "Want me to walk with you?"

"No, no." George wanted to be by himself for a while. "I'll be fine."

Before anyone could suggest an alternative, George left the brewery. He abandoned his tea; the cup material had been bothering his fingers. Leaving it made one less sensory aggravation for him to deal with.

Bumble trundled along behind him. George started out at a quick pace, then slowed down halfway to his cottage; the overwhelming urge to scream or hop up and down had begun to fade away.

A meltdown hopefully averted. George found if he could remove himself from the worst of the sensory avalanche, it often helped immensely. He was grateful for loved ones who didn't press him to stay or insist on going with him. When he needed to be alone, nothing else was going to help.

They were a few minutes from the cottage when Bumble flopped down and refused to walk another step. George hefted him up and carried him the rest of the way. The elderly pug panted happily from his arms.

George rubbed his face against the top of Bumble's head. "Poor wee old man. Don't worry. We'll get you some cold water and a snack. Would you like that?"

There was a massive amount of relief when his cottage came into view. George had to resist the urge to run. He didn't want to jostle poor Bumble too much.

Stepping inside the cottage was almost like being

gently lowered into a massive, soft pile of cushions. The quiet and warmth surrounded him. He set Bumble down and wasn't surprised when he immediately found the first available dog bed to dive into.

"You sorted, then?" George set a clean bowl of water in front of the bed and dropped a handful of treats beside it. "There you go. Snacks in bed."

Sitting on the floor, George leaned against the side of the couch and rested his hand on Bumble's head. He lightly scratched behind the pug's ears. With his eyes closed, he forced himself to take a few slow, deep breaths.

It didn't help.

It did help, but it didn't.

His mind felt like it was swirling around like a tornado. George opened his eyes to avoid the sensation overwhelming him. He counted his breaths, using them as something to focus on instead of his spiralling thoughts.

Is Cara the killer? If she isn't, why has she latched on to me like I was involved? If she is, am I a distraction?

Or is she hoping I'm a distraction?

Oh my days.

I have to stop thinking about this for five seconds.

After communing with Bumble for a while,

George finally got to his feet and went into the kitchen. The spiralling had stopped. He grabbed one of the chai blends his parents had brought him, then hunted in the cabinet for one of his honey syrups.

A nice chai sweetened with raspberry thyme honey syrup would do wonders for him. George stood in the kitchen, swirling a spoon in the tea absently. He was almost mesmerised by the movement of the liquid in the mug.

George was starting to feel the tension bleed off when his doorbell rang. For the hundredth time this summer, he contemplated removing it entirely. "Let's go see who's at the door."

Bumble followed him through the cottage to the front door. George somehow wasn't surprised to discover it was Polly who'd rung the bell. She shifted uncomfortably from one foot to the other while wringing her hands repeatedly.

"Hello." George managed a slightly friendly sounding greeting when all he wanted to do was slam the door in her face. "Can I help you?"

"I just... needed someone to talk to." Polly shoved her hands into her pockets and then yanked them out again. "Could I come in, please? I'd like to apologise for all of this mess."

Not again.

TWELVE

MURPHY

It took all of Murphy's strength not to chase after George. He knew his boyfriend needed space. So, they stayed at the brewery, watching him walk away.

"I'll give him a couple of hours to decompress before I go check on him," Murphy promised Margo, who stared worriedly after her cousin. "He'll be fine."

"Aside from the grieving widow, who keeps attacking him?" Teagan's unhelpful addition didn't settle any of their nerves. They smiled when both Margo and Murphy glared at them. "Am I wrong?"

"No. I'll give him an hour, then check on him." Murphy could swing by the cottage just to make sure everything was okay.

They went into the brewery together. Murphy found it hard to stop worrying about George. The situation was unnerving.

Walking over to the pub, Murphy decided to check on his brother and sister-in-law. They were still setting things up for the next tasting event. The show had to go on despite losing a batch of mead; they always made multiple flavours at one time for that very reason.

Graeme was nowhere to be seen, but Maisie was on a ladder attempting to change one of the wall decorations. She had a wrought-iron tree dangling from one hand while she tried to grab a frame with the other. Murphy rushed across the room to help when she lost her grip.

"What the devil are you doing?" Murphy sighed. Maisie and Graeme were chaotic at the best of times. They had massive hearts but tended to dive headfirst into life without assessing risks. "Where's your lesser half?"

"He had to go pick up supplies in Keith for me." Maisie snickered. She managed to get the frame off the wall, handing it to him and taking the tree to hang up. "There. Perfect. Fits in with the moody, mystical theme. We're inching closer to autumn. I'm ready for summer to be over with, so why not set the season off right?"

A shout drew both their attention. Murphy helped Maisie down from the ladder before racing outside. It was like the most bizarre Highland version of *Groundhog Day* to find Jimmy Larkin yelling in front of the brewery.

What was with the entire family? Murphy had heard weddings brought out the worst in people, but this seemed to be taking things to the absolute extreme with a murder, assaults, and more yelling than a reality show on the telly.

"Where is he? Where's the little bastard who got my sister locked up?" Jimmy started towards Murphy but stopped when he refused to back down. "Where is he?"

"You need to calm yourself down." Murphy had had enough of the Larkins feeling as if they could lay their hands on people. "Your sister put her hands around his throat. George had no control over the police deciding to bring her in for questioning. I imagine they'll be wanting to know if she put her hands on her wife as well. She seems violent."

"Cara would never hurt Val. She loved her. No idea why." Jimmy sneered, though Murphy wasn't sure what it was directed at. He muttered a few choice words about Valerie under his breath. "She was never good enough for my sister. Never. Nothing but trouble. The whole family."

Patience had never been his greatest trait, but Murphy tried his best. The almost petulantly childish way everyone connected to Valerie Collins's death behaved was exhausting. They were all adults.

Gesturing wildly, Jimmy seemed for a moment like he might lunge forward. Murphy stood his ground. He squared his shoulders, which gave the other man second thoughts.

"What exactly did Valerie do?" Maisie stayed behind Murphy, out of reach of the clearly angry man. "You obviously dislike her. Why? All I've heard you say was she was trouble."

"She was."

"What does 'trouble' mean?" Maisie prompted when Jimmy didn't elaborate. "It could be anything at all."

Jimmy mumbled to himself for a moment. "She just wasn't good enough."

"Solid argument." Maisie spoke quietly enough for only Murphy and Teagan to hear her. "I'm dazzled by the depth of it."

"Maisie." Murphy hadn't made up his mind about Jimmy Larkin. He didn't want him lashing out because of a teasing comment. "Why don't you and Teagan check on the mead?"

Out of the corner of his eye, Murphy caught Teagan holding their phone out. He nodded subtly, hoping Jimmy hadn't noticed. At this rate, he couldn't help wondering if Elwin would wind up quitting and running away to the North Pole to avoid them.

Maybe a slight exaggeration.

They definitely weren't putting themselves on his "nice" list. Murphy had hoped Jimmy was winding down from his ranting, but he'd begun to pick up steam again.

The ranting kept going and going. Murphy could barely understand one word in five. Jimmy was like a rocket that had finally been lit and released.

Behind Jimmy, Murphy spotted Elwin's vehicle coming up the lane towards the brewery. Teagan had obviously gotten a hold of him while the detective inspector was still in the village. If he'd been home in Keith, the journey would've taken him more than a matter of minutes.

"Mr Larkin, I'm not sure what you're expecting

me to do about any of this." Murphy tried one last time to calm him down. "I'm not a detective. I wasn't at the scene of the murder. And I didn't entice your sister to launch herself at George."

"All this sodding fuss over a dead twit nobody cared about." Jimmy spat the words out. He waved his hands, causing Murphy to lean away to avoid being smacked. "She doesn't matter."

"Her family cares about her." Murphy caught Elwin's eye over Jimmy's shoulder. "They cared about her. She mattered to them."

"Did she? I doubt it. Polly didn't care when she smashed a rock over her head. Family," Jimmy scoffed. "They didn't care about her, did they?"

"Polly? How do you know that?" Murphy tried to keep Jimmy talking until Elwin decided to intervene. "They're not sure how Valerie Collins died."

"I saw her do it."

The smile on Jimmy's face was disconcerting. Murphy almost recoiled from him. It was a vicious and angry expression.

"You saw Polly kill Valerie? Why didn't you tell the police?" Murphy couldn't help asking, though he expected he knew the answer.

"Why? Not my job, is it?"

The absolute selfish disdain for a life that had been lost was sickening. Murphy wasn't surprised. Jimmy hadn't shown anything but distaste for his dead sister-in-law.

"Mr Larkin?" Elwin finally made his presence known. He came up behind Jimmy, placing a firm hand on his shoulder. "Perhaps you wouldn't mind coming to have a more formal discussion with me—on the record? You seem to have left out a few things when we spoke previously."

"Bumble?"

Murphy glanced around at Teagan's concerned shout. They'd come out of the brewery with Maisie after Elwin had calmed things down. "Bumble?"

"Look." Teagan pointed to where Murphy could see an exhausted Bumble collapsed on the ground. "What the hell? Where's George? He'd never leave him."

Murphy jogged over and crouched down to lift the weary pug into his arms. He was panting heavily and began pawing at Murphy's chest. "Teagan? Can you take him? Get him some water."

"Paddy?" Elwin had left Jimmy standing by his vehicle. "Where's George?"

"I don't know." Murphy grabbed his phone and

tried texting first, then calling George with no answer. "I have a more worrying thought."

"Yes?"

"Where's Polly?" Murphy tried again and again to reach George. "He's not answering."

"We shouldn't jump to conclusions." Elwin was a voice of calm that Murphy had no interest in listening to. "Paddy. You don't know anything's wrong."

"Bumble wouldn't leave George alone for anything. Not to trek all the way here." Murphy gave up trying to call. He pulled his keys out of his pocket, glancing up when Maisie joined him. "Let's go."

"Graeme's on his way as well." Maisie was tapping away at her phone non-stop. "We're reaching out to everyone in the village."

"Paddy."

"See you there." Murphy completely ignored Elwin. He didn't know if they had time for the cautious approach. "He'd answer his phone. And there's no sodding way he'd let Bumble run all the way here on his own."

"I'm coming. Margo's staying with the pups. Bumble's still frantic." Teagan slipped into the back seat before Murphy had even gotten the vehicle started. "Are we just pretending the police aren't trying to get our attention?"

Murphy could see Elwin speaking into his phone while also waving wildly at them. "We're going to the cottage."

We may not have time to wait.

THIRTEEN

GEORGE

Polly made him uncomfortable. Most people did. But something about her made him feel exceptionally uneasy, so much so that he didn't want her in his private space.

"Can I come in?" Polly repeated her question when the silence between them had stretched to several awkwardly long minutes. "Please?"

"No."

Polly blinked at his short answer. She didn't seem to have expected a rejection. "All I'd like to do is apologise."

"Okay. You don't have to come into my cottage to do so. And I don't need one in the first place." George stepped outside with Bumble at his feet. He didn't want to give her a chance to weasel her way into the cottage. He kept the door to his back. "There's nothing for you to apologise for."

She canted her head to the side, seeming slightly twitchy at his response. "If I could just come inside and explain."

"I'm having a quiet day to myself." George refused to budge. Confrontation made him incredibly uneasy, but he didn't want her in the cottage. "You've apologised, so there's nothing else to say."

"What did you see?" Polly reiterated the question she'd posed previously.

"What?" George wished he had his phone in his pocket. "You asked me that earlier. I still don't know what you're talking about."

"What did you see that night? When Valerie died?"

"Other than a lump in the street? It was dark. All I saw was a body in the lane." George found her hyper-focus on what he'd seen disturbing. "Why does it matter? There's nothing I could've done to save her. I came on the scene long after whatever happened to her."

"You saw something. I'm sure you did."

"How?" George had a sudden sinking feeling. He knew exactly why Polly had become so focused on if he'd seen something. "How are you sure?"

"You had to have."

"I didn't." George kept a close eye on her body language. He wasn't brilliant at reading the intentions of others, but he didn't like how tense she was. She kept reaching into her pocket. "And I'd know."

"I know you saw something." Polly kept repeating her accusation over and over.

"I didn't." George frowned as she shook her head in a vigorous refusal to hear him. "I wasn't there when it happened... but I think you were."

Polly froze briefly before yanking her hand out of her pocket. It wasn't empty this time. She held a small pistol, pointing it directly at his head. "I was. I had to follow her just in case."

"In case what?"

"In case I had to hit her again," Polly hissed.

"Why?" George wondered if he had time to get into the cottage and lock the door. He didn't think he stood a chance with her holding the pistol. He had to be patient and keep her talking. "Why did you do it?"

"Perfect Valerie with her perfect life and her perfect job and her perfect girlfriend. Perfect. Perfect. *Perfect*." Polly spoke like a disturbed record on repeat. "And what about me? Pathetic Polly. The little cousin who trailed along after her."

"I'm sure—"

"They laughed at me." Polly waved the gun in his face. "They *laughed* at me. And she was so happy."

The bitterness in her voice was shocking. George reared back to avoid the barrel smacking into his cheek. He tried to nudge Bumble out of the way, not wanting to risk his beloved pug being in danger as well.

To his surprise, Bumble took off down the lane. He'd never gone off alone without George being close behind. It was a relief, at least, to have him out of the line of fire.

Now he just had to get himself away from her. Somehow.

"I know you saw her."

"Well, yes. I saw her in the lane after she'd been struck. I didn't see the attack." George tried to figure out the safest way to get away from her. He didn't like his odds. Maybe he could talk her into letting him go. Or at least convince her to lower the gun. "I haven't the foggiest idea of what happened before the moment my dog sniffed her out."

"Liar." She poked him in the face with the barrel of the weapon. "You're lying."

"I'm not, actually," George stammered indignantly. Now likely wasn't the best time to argue with a gun-wielding murderer, but he couldn't stop himself. "There's video evidence of when I left my cousin's cottage. It's all on film. Well, is it technically film if everything is digital now?"

Not the point, George, not the point.

Now is not the time to argue semantics.

Polly seemed baffled by his rambling. She lowered the gun a little so it was now pointed at his chest instead of his face. "What are you on about?"

"The time I left Margo's cottage was recorded. I couldn't have seen who struck Valerie. I don't have x-ray vision." George shifted forward and to the right, trying to move away from the front door. He didn't want to be trapped in the little alcove at the front of his cottage. There was no place for him to dive or dodge or run. "The only people in the lane that night were myself, your cousin's body, and my pug."

There was a long moment of silence. Polly didn't appear to know how to process what he said. She paced a short circuit on the path, two steps right, then two left. George used her momentary distraction to inch further away from her; she didn't notice while muttering to herself and waving the pistol around.

Trying not to draw attention to himself, George

sidestepped around her until he was no longer trapped against the cottage. Polly kept arguing with herself about what he'd seen. Her fixation on it continued to baffle him.

What did it even matter? George hadn't seen anything. The police hadn't even considered him a witness to anything other than the position of the body.

For the second time over the summer, George found himself having to contemplate his own mortality. He wasn't enjoying the experience. He wondered absently if anyone would mind if he built a moat around his cottage, complete with a draw-bridge; maybe that would be enough to stop murdering twits from harassing him.

Maybe a moat was extreme.

Maybe now's not the time to consider extreme home safety measures while the gun's still pointed in my direction.

Maybe.

"What are you doing?" Polly swung around towards him. "Where are you going?"

"To pull a stray weed." George immediately crouched down and plucked one of the wildflowers out of the garden. He hefted it up as if it were a completely reasonable thing to have done. "See?

Important to keep on top of these things. My bees can't thrive if I don't."

"I... what?"

With running not a safe option, George decided his best bet was to confuse her. If he kept Polly derailed with nonsense, it might keep him safe long enough for help to arrive. Bumble hadn't returned, so all he could hope was he'd gone to either Margo or Murphy.

They'd realise something was wrong. They'd have to. He thought he could hear his phone ringing from inside the cottage, so it boosted his confidence that help was on the way.

"Weeds are bad for bees." George had never lied confidently in his life. He was terrible at it, but he hoped Polly was too bewildered to notice. "Pollinators are important."

"What is the point of this?"

"You asked what I was doing." George lifted the poor flower that he'd sacrificed in order to help save his life. "I'm plucking weeds. There's quite a few. I've been busy in the back garden, so things have gotten away from me here."

"I'm holding a pistol." Polly pointed it at him.

"I'm aware. I can see it." George crouched down and grabbed at a second flower, promising to replant it if possible. "Right there. In your hand. It's quite prominent in my mind."

It was, in fact, all George could think about. He was becoming a little too intimately acquainted with the barrel of a gun for his peace of mind. All he wanted was for it and for her to disappear.

"You're trying to distract me."

I'm trying to live, you absolute....

George considered his odds of being able to disarm her. They made it seem relatively easy in movies. He decided to turn her question around on her. "What is the point of this?"

"What?" Polly was derailed from her continued rant.

"What is the point... of this?" George gestured towards her pistol. He'd continued to move a little at a time, putting himself in hopefully a better position to do something. He just had to figure out what "something" was. "Why come here?"

"You saw something."

"I didn't. But say, for the sake of argument, I did. I've already had my interview with the police. What is coming here going to do?" George hoped he could convince her to leave. "You're only going to make things more difficult for yourself. Why not leave?"

"I can't," she insisted.

"Why not?"

"You're a witness. That's how this works. If there's no witnesses, I'll be safe. They can't arrest me without evidence. I read a book." Polly glowered at him. "Stop moving. I read about this. No witnesses. It's the perfect crime. And if I'm not involved, I'll get the money. No one ignores you if you have money."

"I thought you didn't know about the will?"

"I knew."

George frowned before inching further way from her. "People are going to know you came here, so they'll know you're involved."

FOURTEEN

MURPHY

For being a short distance, the drive to the cottage felt like an absolute eternity. Murphy was exceeding the speed limit beyond what was probably safe. He had to get to George.

"Still no answer." Teagan had continued to try to reach George. "Maybe his phone's in the house while he's in the garden?"

Maisie nodded in agreement. She was still on her phone, coordinating the village response. "I've done it often enough."

In the rear-view mirror, Murphy spied several police vehicles. They'd obviously decided not to wait around. Elwin was probably still cursing his name.

They'd just passed Margo's cottage when a woman ran by at full tilt. Murphy frowned. He kept

going, though, intent on reaching George. She was someone else's problem.

"Was that Polly?" Teagan twisted around to try and get a better look. "One of the constables stopped to try and catch her."

"I don't care," Murphy muttered. George hadn't been with her. "She's not my problem."

"There he is," Maisie stated the obvious.

They could all see him. George was sitting in the middle of his front garden. His right hand tightly gripped his left arm, sending a shiver of fear up Murphy's spine.

Murphy slammed on his brakes, skidding to a stop. He barely remembered to put the vehicle in Park before leaping out and racing over to George. "Are you hurt?"

George didn't lift his head, but he nodded towards his arm. "It burned. I didn't expect that. Like someone punched me with a hot iron."

"Maisie? Call the doc. We're driving him to the hospital." Murphy knew they'd be faster than waiting for an ambulance. "How badly are you hurt?"

"Not a sodding clue." George refused to move his hand to show them the wound. "I can't... deal with gushing blood again."

The evidence of blood was all over the sleeve of his jumper. His fingers were covered. Murphy found it hard to look at it.

"Fair enough." Murphy assessed the situation for a second before crouching down to lift him up. He carried George as gently as possible to the vehicle, where Maisie had the door open. "No time for chats, Elwin. We're going to the hospital. If you have questions, you know where we'll be."

"There's a pistol in the flowers somewhere. I knocked it out of her hand." George grimaced when he had to scrunch up to get into the seat. "I couldn't give her a chance at a second shot. I might not survive it."

"I'm sure Detective Inspector Smith can find the weapon and take care of it." Murphy closed the door and spun around. "Right? You can take care of the *police* matters."

Elwin took a step back when confronted by Murphy's obvious upset. "Easy, Paddy. I'm on your side, remember? We'll follow you to the hospital, ensure you get there okay. I've already gotten a call from Sarah. They've caught Polly Collins."

Murphy gave a sharp nod. He raced around the vehicle and got inside, barely taking time to pull on his seatbelt before gunning the engine. "Hold on."

"You know, it's not Elwin's fault, Paddy." George grimaced over every bump in the road despite Murphy's attempts to keep the ride smooth. His hold on his arm never wavered, even when he slid a little on the seat when they rounded a corner. "We certainly haven't made their job any easier."

They lapsed into silence. Murphy focused on the drive while Teagan and Maisie tried to keep George from sliding around too much. He clenched his teeth tighter with every pained hiss from his boyfriend.

One of the doctors and several nurses were already outside waiting on them. They had George out of the vehicle before Murphy had even said a word. He sat in front of the hospital emergency entrance, unsure how to process the past hour or so.

"Paddy?" Maisie had remained in the vehicle while Teagan darted after George. "Come on. Why don't you park over there? We should go inside."

"I...."

"George is going to be fine. From what I managed to see, the bullet grazed his arm. It's not deep. Yes, there was a lot of blood, but that happens when you're shot." Maisie shifted forward, resting her arms on the tops of the seats in front of her. "He'll want you with him."

"I know." Murphy couldn't shake a slight feeling

of guilt. He wasn't responsible, but it was there none-theless. Maisie gave his shoulder a light pat of support. "Could you give Margo a call? I'm sure she'll want the details."

"I will. I imagine she'll head to the cottage since she has the pups," Maisie promised. "Go on. Let's get out of the way of the entrance."

Pulling forward, Murphy parked the vehicle. He left the keys in the ignition since Maisie wanted to make a few calls. She promised to turn it off and head inside the hospital when she was finished.

One of the nurses was waiting for him by the door. She led him through the building to the room where they were patching up George. Maisie's assessment had turned out to be correct; the bullet had thankfully only grazed him.

The irritated scowl on George's face would've been endearing and humorous under other circum-stances. He was clearly trying to be cooperative but obviously found the hospital experience overwhelm-ing. Teagan nodded to Murphy when he went to stand by them.

All of the adrenaline that had coursed through Murphy vanished. He made it over to a chair against the wall, collapsing onto it when his legs went out from under him. It was all he could do to remember how to breathe.

One of the nurses came over to check on him. She grabbed his arm, lifting it and placing two fingers on his wrist. He assured her he was fine; it had been a rather stressful afternoon.

Just a wee bit of stress.

It seemed like the greatest understatement to have ever been uttered. *Just a stressful afternoon.*

After ensuring his pulse rate was fine, she returned to hovering around the doctor and George. They'd cleaned his wound and were now carefully wrapping it up while giving him care instructions.

Murphy could see George was completely over-whelmed and likely not hearing a word the doctor said. "Doc? Could you write those instructions out for us? I'd hate to miss a step and have him back in here for one reason or another."

George nodded when the doctor glanced between them. "Please."

"I'm making notes," Teagan chimed in from their corner of the room. They were tapping away at their phone. "If it's easier for everyone, I can text the instructions."

"We'll make a paper copy as well," one of the nurses readily assured everyone.

The doctor continued to finish wrapping up George's arm. The instructions were repeated for a second time, but Murphy could see his boyfriend had reached his limit of dealing with everything.

Murphy pushed himself to his feet. He was pleased to see his breathing had returned to normal, leaving him feeling fine. "Can we take him home?"

"As long as he rests and the police are good with it, he's fine to go. We've got a prescription for him— I'll include details in our written instructions." He pulled off his gloves and dropped them into a nearby hazardous waste bin in the far corner of the room. "I want you to take it easy for the next few days at least. Make sure you keep the wound clean and covered."

After giving a few more instructions, the doctor left. Teagan and Maisie followed the nurses out to get all the information for George. He sat on the bed, staring down at his hand.

"George? You want a hand getting up?" Murphy didn't want to overwhelm him any further. He could already see the strain. "George?"

George had his hand out in front of him, fingers spread as wide as they could go. "Paddy. I need your help."

"What's wrong?" Murphy rushed over. He'd been trying to keep a little space between them. His eyes dropped down to George's hand. Dried blood covered his fingers. "Let's get you washed up."

"Okay." George didn't pull away when Murphy held his elbow gently. He allowed himself to be led to the loo connected to the room. It was a tight squeeze, but they both fit inside. "Okay."

"That's right. You're going to be okay. They got you all stitched up. The police have the horrible human detained." Murphy kept one arm around George for support. "And everyone who loves you is going to make certain you recover."

"Just a flesh wound." George managed a weak smile.

"Even those can be scary." Murphy had to use all of his strength to keep from collapsing in relief. He was beyond grateful that nothing worse had happened. "Terrifying, in fact."

FIFTEEN

GEORGE

Murphy's hands were gentle as he helped wash the blood away. George struggled to pull himself out of what seemed like the worst sort of fever dream. An out-of-body experience that he'd had no control over.

The sticky, dried mess on his fingers irritated him. He loathed the sensation. His skin crawled whenever he moved his hand even slightly.

"Easy now, George. We'll get this manky mess off you in no time at all." Murphy worked up a decent lather of suds, then methodically massaged soap over his fingers. He guided them underneath the warm water, allowing the stream to rinse everything away. "Need another round, or are you feeling better?"

"Another."

"All right." Murphy continued to quietly murmur reassurances to him while soaping up his hands for a second time. "We can use the whole bottle. I don't mind."

"They might."

"Sod 'em." Murphy shrugged. "I'll buy the hospital a crate of hand soap. The fancy stuff so they won't whinge at us."

The image made George smile. He appreciated Murphy's calm and measured approach. There was no flinching away from any of it.

A thought occurred to George after the third round of soap. Margo had to know what had happened. If she did, it would likely have travelled through the family.

"Odds of my family descending on Dufftown within the next few hours?"

"High." Murphy grabbed a towel and dried off both their hands. "Why don't we get you home and settled? All cosy at the cottage. I'll make one of your chais. I'm sure we can get something to eat if you're hungry."

"Not volunteering to fight off the family?"

"I'd step in front of a train for you, but I'm not stopping your dad and mum. The Sheths might be too much even for me." Murphy slipped his arm around George again, somehow avoiding jolting his injury while offering his strength. "Let's get you out of here."

"Did they catch her?" George hadn't realised how much he used his arm until he had to purposefully keep from moving it. He was terrified of reinjuring himself or getting an infection. Once he had the written instructions, he'd read them over a few times. "This is going to be such an annoyance."

"Polly?"

"Trying not to move my arm or think about it." George couldn't shake the sensation of his skin pulling. It was going to drive him absolutely batty until he was healed. "I need a distraction."

"We'll get you in your garden. You can watch the bees." Murphy helped him out of the room.

"Why am I so...?" George had only hurt his arm, but he felt like his entire body was on shaky ground.

"Shock. I had a moment myself. You'll feel better once we get you home." Murphy led him towards Teagan and Maisie, who were waiting for them by the exit. They were chatting with Constable Bettley. "Natalie. How's your gran?"

"Good. She's looking forward to your next event." Natalie often brought her grandmother to the brewery. She turned her attention to George, checking him over to see how he was doing. "We found the pistol—without damaging your lovely garden any more than it was. And I was telling these two that Polly Collins has been arrested. I can't give you too many details, but she did confess to murdering her cousin."

"Well, that's something." Murphy broke the silence that had begun to build while everyone stared at George. He hadn't known what to say, so he was happy to let his boyfriend handle it. "Do they need us for anything, or can we head to the cottage?"

"The detectives haven't said anything. I'll make the executive decision to send you all home. Have some tea. My gran heard about George getting shot, so it's all over the village. Everyone wanted to help." Natalie held a hand up to stop everyone from interrupting her. "I had a word. They won't be descending on the cottage en masse. But they did send a delivery of food, so you won't have to worry about making yourself meals for weeks, I imagine."

"Wonderful." George had a feeling he'd sounded more sarcastic than intended. He couldn't bring himself to care. "Someone else can handle them. I'm never answering the door ever again as long as I live."

He was joking. Mostly. Answering the door had

never been high on his list of enjoyable events. It stressed him almost as much as a ringing phone or a full email inbox.

"We'll train Bumble to answer for us." Murphy kept the conversation light, thankfully, since George didn't have the energy to filter his thoughts. He didn't want to be unkind. "And we'll install one of those Ring doorbells like Margo has."

"Probably a wise idea," Natalie agreed. She glanced around at the four of them. "Off with you. Looks like it might rain, so get home before the clouds descend on us. Margo was at your cottage when I left, so you can get all the pug cuddles to cheer you up."

A slow nod was the only response George could manage. He was grateful when Murphy said, "Thank you and goodbye," on his behalf. His capacity for being polite and engaging in small talk had been exceeded. He wanted tea, his pug, and his garden, maybe some music.

Mostly George wanted to sit somewhere comfortable without being required to expend any effort at all. He settled for being helped out to the vehicle despite being completely capable of walking. The strength and warmth of Murphy's arm around him was reassuring.

The drive back to his cottage was far less chaotic and far less painful. George didn't remember much about the ride to the hospital. He'd been too lost in the burning pain in his arm and the pounding in his head. Nothing else really registered to him until he'd had a moment to breathe while waiting for the doctor.

Closing his eyes, George leaned against Murphy, who'd gotten into the back seat with him. Teagan had been handed the keys and done a wonderful job of driving slowly and carefully. They pulled up outside his cottage in what felt like the blink of an eye.

"I may have accidentally told your mum." Margo met them at the door with a dog under each arm. She kept a tight hold of them when Bumble began to wiggle. "I didn't want you tripping over them. They were worried about you."

George wanted nothing more than to reach out and take Bumble, but his injury made it impossible. He didn't want to drop his beloved pug. "Poor wee Bumble Bee. I can't believe you ran all the way to the brewery."

"A proper little hero." Margo set both dogs down once George had gotten into the cottage. "We'll have to give him an extra special treat."

"I need an extra special treat." George decided to

head through the cottage into the garden. He needed to commune with the calmest part of his world. "I have to sit down."

Making his way out into the back garden, George almost burst into tears. Margo had moved blankets and a few pillows out to his favourite chair. He could hear music playing inside the cottage. His preferred mug sat on the little wrought-iron table with a plate of biscuits and pastries.

"Margo." George wanted to throw his arms around her but remembered his injury at the last minute. "Thank you."

Grabbing her arm with his uninjured hand, George gave it a squeeze of thanks. He went over and gingerly lowered himself into the chair. The cushions helped a great deal, particularly when he managed to prop one underneath his wounded limb.

Though his cousin was trying not to fuss, Margo still tucked a blanket around him. She adjusted the pillows behind him and under his arm. Before stepping back, she slipped the case for his earbuds into his hand.

"There's tea. Biscuits. We'll keep your parents from peppering you with questions," Margo promised. She left him alone with Bumble and Treacle, who'd already cuddled up together at his feet. "You can tell us about your adventure later."

In a matter of seconds, George found himself alone with his bees and the two dogs for company. He slipped in his earbuds, not surprised to find Margo had queued up one of his preferred gardening podcasts. The two hosts had soothing voices; it was calm, quiet, and all about his favourite subject.

Despite his best efforts, George couldn't stop thinking about what had happened. The slight twinging in his arm didn't help. He kept his eyes open because he was haunted by visions of the gun when he closed them. It had all happened so quickly, yet each second had been etched forever in his mind.

"George?"

He turned his head to see Murphy hovering off to his right. "Yeah?"

"Want some company?"

"Yeah." George nodded slowly. He'd usually want to be alone, but Murphy was different. "Parents arrive yet?"

A full sentence seemed far too much effort. Murphy wouldn't mind. He didn't take things like that personally.

"Not as yet. Margo gave them a call. They're on their way. She told your dad to drive slowly. He seems to have understood. Prepare yourself, because my dad decided to come with them." Murphy took the seat beside him. He was immediately inundated by the dogs, who wanted up in his lap. "Hello, you two. Are you keeping our George company? Making sure he's doing all right?"

"Hopefully, your mum will keep the Duncan and Rishi show from getting out of control." George usually appreciated how their dads got along so well. But right now, he didn't have the capacity to deal with their chaos. "I know they mean well...."

"But too much for you to process?" Murphy finished the sentence for him admirably.

"Exactly."

Murphy was silent for a while before breaking the quiet. "Do you want to talk about it?"

"Not particularly." George shifted his arm without thinking and immediately groaned in pain. "Making a note to myself not to move my injured wing for a few days."

"Pain meds?"

"Help if I don't bash it around." George sank further into the cushions, thankful for the extra softness. "I wasn't trying to get the weapon or anything. She was calming down but then went from zero to a hundred in a second. I tried knocking her arm to the side as she fired. Think that's why it hit me where it did. The pistol went flying, and she took off running. Not sure she actually intended to hurt me."

"She intended something if she had it pointed at you." Murphy was scowling harder than normal. "I...."

"My son." Rishi Sheth rushed out of the cottage despite them hearing Margo behind him trying to slow him down. "Where are you?"

"Abba."

"My son." Rishi was immediately crouching beside his chair.

"Abba." George tried to mollify his father, who kept petting him lightly on the cheek, scanning him for visible injuries. He'd expected the joyful chaos of Rishi Sheth with his best mate Duncan Baird. "Abba? I'm okay. The injury isn't too bad."

"You were shot."

"Just in my arm." George gestured towards it. His father didn't stop patting him on the cheek. "Where's Mum?"

"You won't distract me with her." Rishi sat back on his heels. He picked up George's uninjured hand and clutched it in both of his. "You're okay?"

"I'm okay. It twinges a bit when I move. But the bullet only grazed my arm." George managed some semblance of a smile for his father. He was relieved when Duncan joined them in the garden. His mum came up behind him. She offered him a knowing grin, well aware of how dramatic her husband could be. "I'm all right."

"'Course you are." Duncan dragged Murphy into a hug. He practically pulled him off his feet, which made George chuckle. "Ahh, my wee bairn. How are you? Are you taking care of our king of the bees?"

"Da." Murphy groaned. "I'm not five years old."

"Behave yourselves. Why don't you three see if Margo needs help sorting out what we're having to eat?" His mum waited for the three men to head into the cottage before coming over to have a seat beside George. "Now, tell me how you're really doing."

"I'm all right." George nudged his foot gently against Bumble, who immediately flopped over onto it with a grumbly sigh. "And he's clearly perfectly fine."

"George."

"Mum." He didn't want to dissect his day a hundred times when he'd barely managed to wrap his mind around it. "I'm not unscathed, but I am okay."

"Good. And your Paddy? Is he taking care of you?"

"He is. We take care of each other." George adjusted the blanket over him a little. "I'll be okay, Mum."

"Of course you will. You've always managed—no matter what life threw at you." She reached over to lightly pat his knee. "I've never doubted your abilities to take care of yourself, darling. But how about you avoid mysteries in the future? Hmm?"

"Yes, Mum, I will do my level best to avoid homicidal strangers who knock on my door in the future." George grinned when she sighed dramatically at him. "I promise."

SIXTEEN

MURPHY

Murphy sipped tea from the mug Margo had slipped into his hand. He kept an eye on George and his mum through the window. They were sitting in silence, from what he could tell. His attention shifted when his dad came to stand beside him. "Da."

"He's good for you."

"Da."

"He is. Makes you less of a grumpy guts in the mornings, according to your brother." His dad threw his arm around his shoulders and gave him a squeeze. "I heard you're moving in with him."

"Graeme needs to quit gossiping," Murphy grumbled. He narrowed his eyes when Rishi Sheth slipped up on his other side. "He's a menace."

"So, you've moved in with my only son." Rishi

pressed in closer, pinning Murphy between the two men. "And you're treating him well?"

"Of course." Murphy tried not to take offence at the question. "We take care of each other."

"He's joking, Paddy."

Murphy grunted a response, focusing his gaze back on George in the garden. "We take care of each other."

Rishi turned towards him. He frowned after observing him for a few seconds. "It wasn't your fault. He would've been in danger no matter what you did or where you were today. He doesn't need your guilt. If you think about it, it won't help either of you in processing what's happened in the past few days or months."

Nodding in understanding, Murphy eased himself out from between the two men. He checked on Margo, who was pottering around in the kitchen. She offered a smile before returning to what she was baking with Teagan's help.

A knock on the door drew all their attention. Murphy set his mug down and went to answer before anyone else. He was somehow not surprised to find Evan on the other side.

"In our defence, we would've called you if George had been questioned by the police." Murphy smirked when Evan simply rolled his eyes at him. "Look at it this way—you could always see if Polly wants to hire you as her solicitor."

"Why are we friends?" Evan pushed by him into the cottage. "Sarah's on her way. I passed her vehicle at Margo's, so I'm guessing she stopped there first."

The cottage was getting a wee crowded for all of the people trying to cram into it. Murphy decided to wait outside for his cousin. He'd expected her to give them a call instead of popping by.

A few minutes passed before Sarah's vehicle came into view. She parked behind Evan's car. Murphy waited for her to join him on the path.

"How is he?"

"Enjoying a quiet moment in the garden with his mum." Murphy slid his hands into his pockets, rocking back on his heels. He stared past his cousin to the horizon in the distance. "He had a close call."

It was hard to be in the front garden and not visualise Polly with her pistol. Murphy knew they'd gotten lucky. The bullet could've easily done more lasting damage than a graze to George's arm.

They'd gotten so very lucky.

Murphy shook himself out of his thoughts when Sarah placed a hand on his shoulder. She gave him an understanding and sympathetic look.

"How are you?" Sarah squeezed his shoulder, then dropped her hand to her side. "Never easy seeing someone you love hurt."

"I'm fine."

"Paddy." Sarah had never been one to mince her words. It was part of what made her such a great detective. "It's okay to not be fine."

Murphy nodded but didn't really have anything else to say about how he was doing. "Any news on Polly?"

"Paddy."

"You can help me by reassuring me that no one's going to be coming after George again." He didn't think either of them would settle until they knew for certain Polly wasn't a danger.

"Paddy, I can't give you the details of an ongoing investigation." Sarah held her hands up when he glared at her. "Easy. I can tell you she's had her initial interview. She made a full confession, so she's not going to be released. They were waiting for the prosecution service to get back to them when I left. But I've no doubt she'll be charged and held in custody. She won't be let out, given what she's admitted to doing. Considering how close I am to you both, I'm not involving myself any further, though I'm sure we'll want an official statement from George at some point."

The news helped Murphy to slowly release the stress he'd been holding. Polly wouldn't be able to hurt anyone else. They were likely free of anyone connected to the murder of Valerie Collins.

"I think we both just want this bizarre summer to be over. Dead bodies keep popping up in the most inconvenient places." Murphy looked tiredly at his cousin. He didn't know what the worst part of the past few months had been, but hopefully, Polly Collins being arrested would put an end to it. "No more dramatic escapes. No more absolute wankers trying to annoy the life out of us."

"Literally and figuratively?"

"Sarah." Murphy couldn't help chuckling when she grinned at him. "All I want is a quiet life with a little less murder. Is that so much to ask?"

EPILOGUE

GEORGE

Several weeks had passed since the final confrontation with Polly. George's arm had healed entirely. His nightmares had slowed to maybe one every couple of weeks; his online therapy appointments had helped him a great deal.

It was the last week of October. Autumn had brought rain. Rain and more rain. George didn't mind since it was all part of the seasonal cycle.

His videos had gone from end-of-summer to-dos straight into preparing both the garden and his hives for the winter. He was slowly becoming more comfortable with being on camera. His vlogs were gaining traction in the little community of beekeepers and gardeners online.

He'd even managed a sponsorship from one of

his favourite supply shops. Margo had taken over some of the business side of things. He paid her, of course, despite her trying to argue him out of it.

Whatever business George built from his garden and hives, Margo had gone above and beyond to help him. If he made money, he wanted her to share in the success. They'd finally managed to work out something they both found fair.

Evan had helped. He'd whinged the entire time about them being the most demanding clients of his career. George was reasonably sure he'd been joking.

They were making massive plans for next spring and summer. George was excited at what his small hobby might turn into. It helped that Murphy had been encouraging him the entire time. His boyfriend had always had faith in him.

But today, George had left his camera at home. He was helping Maisie and Graeme prepare for the Halloween mead-tasting event at the pub. They were doing something extra special around the building itself.

It was supposed to be a surprise for Murphy. And he'd definitely been stunned when he stepped outside to take in the work in progress. George shook his head when Maisie and Graeme immediately fled the scene of the crime with Teagan in tow.

"What do you think?" George gestured to what was a tangled collection of body parts. He bent down to pick up one of the arms, giving it a little wave. "They're not real."

Murphy stared at the corpses in front of the pub side of the brewery. "I distinctly remember saying I wanted fewer dead bodies in our lives. This appears to be more than I ever recall seeing. Was there a reason for this?"

"They're not real." George sent a wicked grin in his direction. "Maisie had an idea."

"That is *not* the bloody point. And of course she did." Murphy glared at him for a second before they both cackled with laughter. "Did you have to go with a zombie apocalypse theme for Halloween?"

"Maisie insisted. I've been helping her get the arms and legs right." George had pulled out his little-used artistic skills to help paint the fake limbs. "We'll put them all around the car park and up the lane leading to the pub."

"I genuinely hoped we were over the dead body thing." Murphy nudged one of the green-tinted arms. He wasn't ordinarily squeamish around what Maisie called "spooky season." "Did it have to be zombies?"

"Call it shock aversion therapy. By the time the

Halloween party is over, you might not even have nightmares about bodies."

"Or have more of them." Murphy shuddered when one of the arms rolled towards his foot.

"Think positively."

"You are remarkably calm about all of this." Murphy launched the arm across the pavement with his foot. They both snickered when it bounced several times before coming to a stop. "That is disturbing."

"I am choosing to enjoy the spirit of the season. The spirit season. Seasonal spirit? What does Maisie call it? Spooky season?" George enjoyed Halloween. He also appreciated Maisie's dramatic celebratory flair. "In all honesty, this is scaled back from her original plans."

"Yet, somehow, it doesn't comfort me at all to know it might've been worse." Murphy sighed. They were both well aware of how Maisie and Graeme amped themselves up while planning brewery events. "Are you still dressing up for the event?"

"My beekeeping kit. Margo knitted Bumble a bumblebee sweater. She's got a matching one for Treacle. So, I'll have my bees around me. Didn't I show you?" George didn't plan on staying at the mead-tasting party for the entire evening. It would be too overwhelming. "Still planning on wearing your kilt?"

They'd chatted about their outfits earlier when it became clear Maisie wanted a fancy dress party atmosphere. Tickets had sold out for the event within a week of them being available. George figured his beekeeping kit would allow him to avoid people if he wanted.

His full kit included the new hat. Instead of a wide-brimmed one, it was more of a hooded fencing-style one. He figured it also made for a better costume.

"Can you imagine Sarah's and Elwin's faces when they see what we've done?" Murphy nudged him in the side. "They're never going to forgive us for this. "Maybe we can get them to come in their old uniforms?"

"I'm not asking." George couldn't hold back his chuckle at the idea. "We'll have Teagan ask. They're less likely to wind up in trouble."

"I'm sure they'll appreciate us foisting it off on them." Murphy crouched down to lift Bumble into his arms. "I see he's wearing the mangled jumper your dad made for him."

"I did promise." George couldn't help smiling whenever he saw it. "Why did my mum think they needed a hobby?"

"It could be worse."

"I suppose. They haven't graduated to making full garments for us yet." George was waiting for the day. "Maybe Christmas."

"You've jinxed us," Murphy groaned.

Their fathers had apparently driven George's mum to absolute distraction. She'd finally enrolled them in a knitting class as a joke. It had backfired when the two men decided to take up the hobby.

"Who knew competitive knitting was a thing?" George had been getting daily videos from his mum. It was entertaining until he'd started getting the fruits of their labour. "The jumper at least resembles what it's supposed to be. The scarf I got the first time was more like a woolly snake gone awry than an actual article of clothing."

"Maybe we can convince them to stick with gifts for Bumble and Treacle." Murphy glanced over at him for a moment. "I don't like our odds."

"No, I don't either." George snickered to himself, imagining what kind of mangled mess might be heading their way next. "Mum's at least happy they're not bothering her anymore."

"Speaking of Sarah."

"We weren't, but okay." George tensed for whatever news Murphy had. "Out with it."

"Polly Collins did wind up pleading guilty to her attack on you... finally. Her barrister managed to convince her that with all the evidence, there was no way to win. She was sentenced in the High Court last week. A mandatory life sentence. She won't be able to hurt you again." Murphy rested a hand firmly on George's shoulder. "Sarah thought we'd want to know."

"So, it's really over?" George had meant it as a statement, but some of his fears came out despite his best efforts. He leaned into Murphy when he slipped his arm around him. "No more worrying about who's at the door?"

"Depends on if you worry about our fathers and friends. They can certainly cause enough trouble." Murphy twisted George around so they were facing each other. He brought his hands up to rest on George's shoulders. They were close enough that their noses touched. "Remember what our therapist said."

"We survived. We're safe. Our little cottage and garden haven't been ruined by a few wasps." George had appreciated the therapist latching on to his love of bees and using it to help him in the healing process. "Just because I'm afraid doesn't mean something dreadful is going to happen."

"Exactly." Murphy drew him into a brief kiss. "We're going to be all right. All we have to do is survive Maisie's zombie obsession."

"What's another dead body?" George tried for a laugh. He grinned when Murphy dropped his forehead on top of his shoulder and chuckled. "At least these ones don't come with a police inquiry."

"Small mercies."

"Do you believe in happy ever afters?"

"I believe in us. I believe in the slow-burning love that we've kindled together." Murphy punctuated each sentence with a kiss. "And I believe in the little home we're building for ourselves and our family. What do you think?"

"I think I'll take the reality of us over fairy-tale endings any day of the week." George smiled against Murphy's lips. "Not to ruin the mood, but can we not do this over a pile of corpses?"

"I can safely promise to kiss you anytime you want—even over a pile of fake zombies."

"Not the most romantic of offers." George couldn't stop grinning at his boyfriend. "But I happily accept."

"We'll drink a toast to kisses and comfort—and

an end to a summer of murder inquiries." Murphy draped his arm across George's shoulders. "And happy endings with or without the fairy tale."

LOOKING for more MM cosy mysteries from Dahlia? Check out two fun series: **The Grasmere Cottage Mystery Trilogy** and **London Podcast Mystery Series.**

ACKNOWLEDGMENTS

A massive thank-you to my brilliant betas who take my first draft and help me turn it into something legible. To Becky, Kristin, and all the fantastic people at Tangled Tree and Hot Tree Publishing. And also to my beloved hubby, who keeps me from losing my mind while I'm stressing over word counts.

And lastly, thank you, readers, for following me on my writing journey. I hope you enjoyed *Honey Moon Murder*.

ABOUT THE AUTHOR

Thanks for reading Honey Moon Murder. I do hope you enjoyed my story. I appreciate your help in spreading the word, including telling a friend. Before you go, it would mean so much to me if you would take a few minutes to write a review and share how you feel about my story so others may find my work. Reviews really do help readers find books. Please leave a review on your favorite book site.

Don't miss out on New Releases, Exclusive Giveaways, and much more!

Join my newsletter:

http://eepurl.com/QonoX

Join my reader group:

www.facebook.com/groups/1108750876162947

I'd love to hear from you directly, too. Please feel free to email me at dahlia@dahliadonovan.com or check out my website https://dahliadonovan.com/ for updates.

Dahlia Donovan wrote her first romance series after a crazy dream about shifters and damsels in distress. She prefers irreverent humour and unconventional characters. An autistic and occasional hermit, her life wouldn't be complete without her husband and her massive collection of books and video games.

 facebook.com/dahliadonovan

 x.com/DahliaDonovan

 instagram.com/dahliadonovanauthor

pinterest.com/dahliadonovan

ABOUT THE PUBLISHER

Tangled Tree Publishing loves all things tangled and aims to bring darker, twisted, and more mind-boggling books to its readers. Publishing adult and new adult fiction, TTPubs are all about diverse reads in mystery, suspense, thrillers, and crime.

For more details, head to www.TANGLEDTREEPUBLISHING.COM

facebook.com/tangledtreepublishing

x.com/ttpubs

tiktok.com/@hottreepublishing

www.ingramcontent.com/pod-product-compliance
Lightning Source LLC
Chambersburg PA
CBHW061448210726
48287CB00007B/2406